MARTHA, JACK
& SHANCO

Martha, Jack
& Shanco

PARTHIAN

Caryl Lewis has published eleven Welsh-language books for adults, three novels for young adults and thirteen children's books. Her novel Martha, Jac a Sianco won Wales Book of the Year in 2005, as did her novel, Y Bwthyn, in 2016. Caryl wrote the script for a film based on Martha, Jac a Sianco, which won the Atlantis Prize at the 2009 Moondance Festival. Her television credits include adapting Welsh-language scripts for the acclaimed crime series, Y Gwyll/Hinterland, and writing for the major rural noir crime drama, Craith/Hidden.

Gwen Davies grew up in a Welsh-speaking family in West Yorkshire. She has translated into English the Welsh-language novels of Caryl Lewis, published as Martha, Jack and Shanco (Parthian, 2007) and The Jeweller (Honno, 2019), and is co-translator, with the author, of Robin Llywelyn's novel, published as White Star by Parthian in 2003. She is the editor of Sing, Sorrow, Sorrow: Dark and Chilling Tales (Seren, 2010). Gwen has edited the literary journal, New Welsh Review, since 2011. She lives in Aberystwyth with her family.

Martha, Jack & Shanco

Caryl Lewis

Translated by Gwen Davies

PARTHIAN

Parthian, Cardigan SA43 1ED
www.parthianbooks.com
First published in 2007
Reprinted in 2020
Welsh Original: Martha Jac a Sianco © Caryl Lewis, 2004
(www.ylolfa.com)
English Translation © Gwen Davies, 2007
ISBN 978-1-912681-77-8
ISBN (ebook) 978-1-912681-78-5
Cover design by Sion Ilar
Typesetting by Elaine Sharples
Printed by 4edge Limited
Translated with the financial support of
Llenyddiaeth Cymru Dramor / Welsh Literature Abroad
The publisher acknowledges the financial support of the Welsh Books Council.
British Library Cataloguing in Publication Data
A cataloguing record for this book is available from the British Library.
Every attempt has been made to secure the permission of copyright holders to
reproduce images.

Tri pheth sy'n anodd nabod,
Dyn, derwen a diwrnod.
Mae'r dderwen yn gou,
a'r diwrnod yn troi,
a'r dyn yn ddau wynebog.

Three things it's hard to fathom,
An oak, the day, a person.
The oak is dry,
The day will die,
The man you can't rely on.

Traditional, translation:
Gwen Davies & Grahame Davies

'Pourquoi? Qui t'a forcee?'
Elle repliqua, 'Il le fallait, mon ami.'

'Why was it? Who drove you to it?'
She replied. 'It had to be, my dear!'

Madame Bovary
Gustave Flaubert

ONE

'Get a bloody move on then, or it'll be light before we get there.'

'C... c... I ca... ca...can't see...'

'Bring that light back here, Jack, for God's sake, or we'll all end up with our legs broken.'

Jack had struck out ahead, taking the torch with him bouncing along the hedgerow as he stumbled up the lane.

'We'll catch the buggers at it. Something's up around here, and I'm tellin' you, God only help 'em once I get hold of 'em.'

Martha watched his figure, backlit by the torch, as it pushed through the darkness. It was pitch black.

'Come on, Jack! We've no proof no one's done anything to her. Could be some calf's getting into the field somehow and suckling her at night.'

'What calf getting in, woman? See sense will you, and don't be so daft. It's that sod next door's fault, isn't it... leavin' the gates open all the time and putting bits of metal in among the hay rows at harvest. Or that Will over the other side. Peas in a pod they are, and I bet they're 'avin' a good old laugh at us right now.'

Martha heard Shanco fretting behind her.

'Come on then Shanco love, keep up now please.'

Jack and Martha reached the top of the dark lane that ran along the yard, splitting Graig-ddu farm into three: the Banc, the Hendre and Macyn Poced. Both leaned against the gate to wait for Shanco who was still struggling through the mud and darkness. Jack had a long poker in one hand for hitting anyone he came across on the head. As they both stared into the night, Martha noticed that the cow in the field had got up. At last Shanco came up behind in his tight green wool cap. From under his jumper his terrier looked out, his little burning black eyes already fixed on the cow.

'Right then, got to take it gentle like, we'll go and hide in the hedge. If anyone sets foot in here I'll 'ave his balls!'

Martha pulled the collar of her coat tighter. Jack opened the gate and all three walked down to the bottom hedge. Jack turned off the torch and the three of them crouched together.

'D... do w... we have to wait here all night?' Shanco stuttered, the cold making his stammer worse than usual. His nose wrinkled as he tried to avoid sitting on a cow pat. Jack gave him a dirty look in reply.

'Move over now then, Jack. I'm sitting on a thistle.'

It was a cold night and the dew was soaking their backsides. The moon stood out like a hole in a corrugated iron roof, though it cast a wan light. The three settled down to watch the cow while she did her best to ignore them.

Jack was the oldest; he was stout and ruddy with a tea cosy on his head. Whenever his fuse got lit, and that was often, there would be an explosion of Rizlas and matches. The only clue that he was past his prime was his limp which inspired the boys from the mart to call him Tick-tock. Well, that and because he was like a bomb ready to go off any minute.

Martha, shivering by Jack's side, was beautiful considering her age: her thick dark hair had kept away most of the grey so far. Shanco was the youngest; he was as thin as a whippet and kept his terrier under his jumper at all times, making his stomach shake like jelly.

It was cold under the hedge and the unwitting cow kept glancing over at them. Now and then Jack would use his sleeve to wipe a drop of water from his nose.

She was a pretty cow too, a little black and white heifer with a velvet udder. But if you looked at her closer you would be struck by something horrific. She only had one teat, and a bloody one at that. It looked as if it were giving the world the finger.

'She must be catching them on the barbed wire somewhere,' Martha suggested quietly to Jack.

'I move her every night. Don't you think I've already thought of that?'

Martha's back was aching since all she had on was her nightie and an overcoat. She'd been dragged from her bed in the middle of the night. She wondered how she could ever get up from this crouching position. Snuffling came from Shanco's direction: he was fast asleep while his little dog licked his ear occasionally. Time slowed right down. Martha noticed how you could see the whole farmland from here. The farm was an odd old shape too; long and narrow with the church one end and the valley the other. She could see the lights of the village beyond the church three miles or so away, and in the other direction the town's glare was seeping orange into the sky. The fields were breathing damply in the night air, and the hedgerows were like veins stretching towards the house. It was dead quiet, as though they were the only three on the planet. Leaves whispered in the hedge and they could hear the loud crunching of the other cattle grazing in the next field.

'*Look*!' Jack jumped as though he'd been shot.

The cow had raised her back leg and was reaching her head back to inspect her udder. Shanco woke up.

'She's looking for her teats,' Martha whispered, taking hold of Jack's arm.

But the cow stretched her muzzle further, towards the last bloody teat, and she sucked it.

The three of them stared in silence at the cow as the light increased around them. She sucked and sucked and she nibbled at it until the only thing connecting the teat to the udder was a thin strip of skin.

'B... b... b... buttttt,' Shanco stuttered to a halt. Jack grabbed the fence and started to pull himself up.

'Never seen anything like it! A cow with a thirst for 'er own milk!' Jack watched Martha trying to get up. 'She's out of her mind. Got to be.'

Martha raised herself awkwardly and then she offered her hand to Shanco who looked tempted to go back to sleep. All three looked at the cow standing quietly as her wet eyes stared right back at them. Somehow the red blood around her mouth stood out more for being against the black and white hair. Martha noticed that the dawn chorus was building up to a crescendo.

'Well, well, what'd Mami have to say about this?'

TWO

It was eight in the morning and Martha had hung last night's coats over the stove. From their warmth seeped a grassy aroma that filled the kitchen. Holding a loaf against her apron, she spread a layer of butter on the cut side and sliced it thinly. Graig-ddu had a long kitchen with a pantry at the back to keep food cool and to salt pork. The pantry was paved with slates that moved as you stepped on them, spitting up water onto your ankles. The orchard came right up behind the house, making it dark and damp; the wallpaper's original light blue a distant memory, since by now it was blackened by smoke.

'What's the fuckin' idiot gone and shot her for?' Jack kicked the cake sacks by the door and went over to the table in dung-covered wellingtons. 'We'll get bugger-all from the Ministry now, the bloody idiot.' The tobacco pouch in his hands was shaking. 'He must be crazy!' Martha carried on frying bacon at the stove, letting the hot fat spatter her hands. 'The old bitch is lying across the milking yard. The cows 'ad to walk over her to get to the parlour this mornin'. She's covered in shit.'

She took note of his flaming cheeks, how the bristles on his neck were like those on a yard brush.

'Calm down now, Jack. You know what Dr Evans said.'

'The hell with Dr Evans! The doctor's the one the lad'll need to see when I've finished with 'im, the daft moron! If he 'ad to shoot her, why couldn't he do it up in the field out of the way?'

She knew that give him ten minutes, he'd run out of steam, and so she gave him his breakfast.

'The lad can't help it. He couldn't stand seeing her in all that pain.'

'Bloody lad? He's over fifty, for God's sake! And another thing: nothing bothered that heifer, she was great.'

He snatched the penicillin bottle in front of him by its neck to get at the ketchup. The table was covered in a mess made up of a sheep marker; cattle tags; old paper, elastics for lambs' tails and a lovely pineapple Martha had seen reduced in the Co-op.

'Where's 'e now then?' Jack asked, yolk dripping down his chin.

'Feeding the calves somewhere.'

'All 'e's fit for.'

She spread more butter on the loaf she was holding. Roy, Jack's sheepdog was shivering at the door. Clearly he wasn't the only one to catch Jack's temper when he'd found the cow.

'Is that man callin' round tonight then? It's Friday night,' Jack asked, still smarting.

'His name is Gwynfor,' Martha replied before slapping the bread onto his plate. 'And I've no idea whether he's coming tonight or not.'

'The world's full of men and you have to choose a wimp?'

'Be quiet, Jack. I don't poke my nose into your business.'

'Got a nice place, mind, other side of the village. Bit younger than you too. Wouldn't do too bad with 'im over there.'

She went to wipe up the crumbs from the oilcloth with a wet dishcloth.

'He's been calling here for years now,' Jack offered more gently.

She had penned in the crumbs at the table's edge and now she pushed them off carefully into her palm.

'Shut up!'

Her fist was closed around the crumbs.

He went back to his bacon and eggs.

'M... M... Martha! B... bo... bo...'

Shanco was at the door, upset and out of breath.

'He... he –'

She saw his dog wasn't under his jumper.

'Where's Bob, Shanco?'

'In th... the h... h... haybarn,' he said, going straight out again.

Martha dried her hands on her apron, then followed him wearily. She leaned against the doorjamb as she pulled on her wellingtons. Jack was still eating.

'Shambles of a dog 'e is too. If he wanted to shoot anyone, 'e should've shot him: right up his fuckin' arse.'

Martha walked quickly over the yard, nursing her back which was aching from their vigil. The haybarn was quiet and she knew what to expect. Seven bodies lay on the ground: four ginger kittens; one tortoiseshell, all colours like fruitcake, and two black ones. All had their mouths open and the fur around their necks was wet. Shanco and Martha knelt awkwardly by their side. Bob, bored by the whole business, was long gone to hunt a rat under some sink somewhere. Shanco was on the verge of tears.

'S... s... sorry, Martha, B... Bob's a bad boy, and sorry for shooting the cow too. Thought maybe she'd b... burst without teats.'

She looked at the small bodies and she picked up each one and placed them in a pile. This way they hardly looked as though anything was wrong with them. She held up the tortoiseshell and looked at its tiny face. The mother cat was miaowing above them from the roofbeams. Shanco was nursing one of the little bodies as if it were a baby.

By now this was one of Bob's old tricks. On the arrival of a new litter he'd jump and bark again and again until the kittens were demented and would fall to the ground and then he would kill them. They weren't in any real danger since they'd be far too high for Bob to reach them but you couldn't explain that to them. Each time every litter met the same fate.

Both of them stared at the bundle for a while until Shanco put down the little body and pulled something from his pocket which he offered to Martha.

'S... s... snowdrop bulbs for you. For the spring.'

THREE

'Come in, come in. Sit down.' Gwynfor came in as he did each time every Friday night. He would put his head in first and after a moment, walk on in. Martha's cheeks were flushed. 'Sit down, we'll have tea now.'

Jack smirked at Gwynfor. Shanco was sitting by the fire nursing a bruised eye, Bob peeping from the top of his jumper with a sulky look.

'It's a lovely night, isn't it?' Gwynfor said.

Jack looked at him. He was rolling his cigarettes ready for the next day. Sat opposite Jack, it was easy to count the differences between them. Gwynfor always wore a tidy grey suit, an open-necked shirt and his shoes shined with Pledge. He was watching Jack string the tobacco in the Rizla paper. *His* nails were thick as a ram's horn. Gwynfor dragged his white hands across the table and hid them out of the way into his lap.

'And how's the world treating you, Jack?'

He tapped each cigarette on the table to trim them.

'Too much work and I'm not getting any younger.'

'Yes, it comes to us all, doesn't it?'

Jack looked at him. 'Yes, and it's worse for a woman some'ow, isn't it?'

Martha banged the frying pan against the stove.

'Well all that work's hard on the bones, isn't it?'

'Specially when you've got no one to 'elp.'

Shanco looked up at Jack in silence. The bruise reached

from the middle of his cheek to his forehead. He went back into his shell.

'Well you've got Martha here to do your paperwork and look after the house. That must be a big comfort to you. I'd say you're lucky.' She was the other side of the kitchen, dishing up. She blushed. 'And talking of women,' Gwynfor said to him pointedly, 'I hear you've got your own lady-friend.'

'And where d'you hear that?' Jack asked, bristling.

'Little bird, you know.'

Martha brought the plates of fried potatoes and bacon to the table. She threw down the cutlery before giving Shanco his small plate by the fire. She poured hot water into the teapot that was warming on the stove, and drops spattered on the hotplate. As she put the teapot on the table, Jack pulled off his hat and gave it to the pot to wear while it brewed the tea. The four ate in silence until she got up to fetch two mugs and two cups and saucers from the dresser. This was where they kept food and tea now, since the fine china it had held had been sold by Jack to some passing tinkers while she'd been out. They would have taken the dresser too, had she not got back in time to send them packing.

'Hear you've been unlucky with some heifer lately too?' Gwynfor suggested as he wiped his plate with bread and glanced at Shanco.

'Looks like you've been hearing quite a bit lately then, eh?' Jack said, sitting back. 'I'd say you know the bloody lot.'

'No, come on. Just heard Jim the Slaughterhouse had to take her away, that's all. No teats left on her at all.'

Martha jabbed a plate of bread and butter in front of Jack. He took a piece without taking his eyes off Gwynfor.

'New breed, see: titless cow. Strange you haven't heard of that, seeing's you know everything.'

She heard Shanco laughing by the fire.

'Shall we have our tea in the parlour, Gwynfor?' she asked.

Gwynfor agreed as he always did. Martha poured the tea and carried the two cups and saucers into the parlour, leaving the mugs behind. He followed, and even though he had been calling at Graig-ddu for over twenty years, he banged his head as usual on the door-frame as he went through the low doorway. Jack was at the table smoking with a faraway look, and Shanco had gone to sleep by the fire, Bob jumping up to lick the grease from his plate.

The parlour was dark like the other rooms at the back, and was decorated with a mounted fox's head. Its thick walls sucked out the room's heat, keeping it the same temperature throughout the year. The recesses of an old range set in the wall gaped open, and the beams above made you feel as though you were inside a carcase. The furniture was heavy, apart from the pink sofa set in front of the old television. The pair sat down as they always did.

'I was thinking of buying a piano,' said Martha suddenly, sitting back on the sofa. Gwynfor's eyebrows went up.

'Piano?'

'Yeah, I want to have a go at learning the piano. Mami said that when she was in service as a little girl over at Treial, she liked playing piano in the drawing room when Mistress'd gone out.'

'Oh!'

'It'd be fun to learn, wouldn't it? Show there's life in us yet.' Her eyes were shining. She always looked forward to Friday nights, being able to sit in the parlour chatting to Gwynfor.

11

'Martha…'

'I could get a book then with all the notes and everything in it; learn it from that. Don't have to have lessons, do I? That old rheumatism hasn't reached my hands yet anyway.'

'Martha…'

'It wouldn't take me long.'

'Martha, I would be very happy if you could tell Jack that I want to marry you.' She went as still as a millpond. 'And have wanted to for years. He thinks I'm a right – well, I don't know what – carrying on calling here but not taking you seriously.'

'Well let him think what he wants. That's how it is.' She closed her fingers tightly round her cup.

'You know we can't go on like this, Martha.'

She seemed to find the arm of the sofa very interesting.

'You know nothing would please me more than you coming to live with me at Troed-rhiw. I know it's too late for us to have children, but we can keep each other company….' She noticed she could see right through the thin china.

Gwynfor put his tea down by the sofa and moved closer to her.

'I can't wait much longer, Martha.'

Her eyes were darkening. The best china was the most fragile.

'What with all that's happened, we know each other pretty well now. I need someone, Martha, someone to grow old… older with.'

'But Mami said…'

'Forget Mami for a minute, can't you?' He kicked his tea over the carpet.

'Oh look, I'll have to mop…'

'Leave it be, Martha… just for a minute, leave it…'

But she was already on her knees mopping the tea with a dishcloth from her apron pocket. He watched her for a while.

'I'd like to put the piano over in that corner,' she said, her voice juddering as she wiped. 'Then I could play for you when you come over.'

Gwynfor closed his eyes and rubbed his head quietly.

'Martha. It isn't fair on you either. You've got to decide.' She was still scrubbing away. He got up and turned to the door. 'Thanks for the meal. I'll call again for your answer. But I won't call for a while mind; give you time to think it over.'

He watched Martha scrubbing quietly before turning on his heels out of the room. Fluff from the carpet had come away in clumps in her cloth, but she carried on scrubbing until her arm ached. Then she stopped and kneeled up. She looked towards the door.

Looking in through the parlour window was Shanco. He'd heard the back door closing and looked over the garden hedge to see Gwynfor getting into his car. He watched the car lights all the way up the lane while Bob ran in circles around his feet.

FOUR

Martha and Shanco leaned on the field gate, watching Jack training his dog. The sheds at the bottom of the yard were full of dogs snuffling under the doors whenever anyone walked past. Today it was Roy's turn to work. He was a happy dog with a big smile, but on duty he seemed mesmerised. He stepped carefully through the grass, his claws as though they were drawing stitches through the earth. His eyes were drawn instinctively to the fat lambs, and his body ran like a thread.

Jack would choose around fifteen fat lambs to work with. These were less greedy and easier for a new dog to handle. The training would start straight after birth. He'd take the dog everywhere with him, let him come into the tractor cab, accompany him on fox shooting trips up the valley. It's strange how a dog has no natural fear. He learns it from watching other dogs. Same is true of nasty dogs, one will tend to copy the next; they learn bad habits from each other. That's why Jack would never keep together two or three the same age. That would be asking for trouble.

About seven months later Jack would walk among the sheep with the dog on a lead. Just showing enough of them to spark curiosity, keeping him on a tight rein. After that the hard work would start. Some of the dogs were hopeless. A dog born daft will stay daft. Only thing to be done then is get rid of it. But Roy was different. He didn't need a lead, even though he was only nine months old. He'd sit at his master's feet yearning to run. Jack looked at the sheep and leaned on his stick. A second's delay and then he shouted, 'Away.' Roy circled around the knot of sheep. '*Sit!*' Roy sat down as though he'd been shot. Jack moved slowly around the sheep again while Roy's eyes darted wildly between them and Jack. 'Come by!' He was up and circling the sheep from the other direction while they trampled the earth and turned at angles. Shanco was smiling at the gate. Jack looked at the dog panting as though Roy was in another world.

He was a sensitive dog, a pedigree Border Collie. Jack knew exactly how to handle him. There was no point raising your voice and shouting at him. The more brains a dog has, the less you need to shout. He was a natural. Jack couldn't stand the way town men kept sheepdogs as pets. He could divine from a look in a town dog's eye and tell that it was going quietly, surely mad. He couldn't imagine a worse life for a sheepdog.

A good dog respects its owner, wants to please him. Border Collies were different from Huntaway dogs and any other breed. Jack had sold a scruffy dark Huntaway the previous year. It was too big, too noisy and it would jump over the sheep. He preferred dogs that moved with grace, with sense. He'd had to beat the Huntaway till it howled like a baby, to show it who was boss. Border Collies, especially the best ones, just didn't need that treatment. He looked over at Shanco by the gate and caught his glance; Shanco lowered his eyes sheepishly.

Jack decided Roy needed a challenge. It was easy enough for him to run the right way when his master was walking round the sheep with him. That didn't prove any talent. Roy was like a pulse at your temple, primed to be off, but Jack made him stay sitting for a second, his pink tongue hanging out of the corner of his mouth, the saliva dripping from it. Then when Jack was ready he strode through the sheep, scattering them. 'Away.' This time the dog would need to show he could remember the different commands. Roy jumped up. Jack tightened his grip on the alcathine pipe in his hand. Shanco and Martha were at the gate, taking turns to breathe in deeply. The sheep were across the field as though unwound from a fraying fleece. Roy smartly ran a sickle shape around them then dropped to his belly. Jack was bang opposite the dog; the sheep once more a tidy ball of wool between them. Jack leaned on his stick and smiled. Roy smiled back at him through the lamb's legs.

FIVE

There was simmering in the saucepans, steaming up the windows. Saucepans and frying pans sat spreading over the whole hotplate while the stove purred underneath. You could hear Jack's old car from outside and Shanco sunk lower in his seat. Over the lino came tap-tap heels.

She was just as Martha had imagined. Younger but ugly. Brazen face and a fake smile. Jack followed her in, telling her to sit down. Shanco wanted to get a proper look but couldn't manage to keep his eyes on her for long enough.

Martha had cleared the table properly and had set it already. It was at times like these that she most missed the best china.

She spoke in English. 'Is there owt I can do, duck?' she asked without the slightest intention of doing anything.

Martha paused then answered, 'No, thank you.'

She poured the potato water into the roasting tin to make gravy. She took the potatoes in their saucepan, together with the masher, over to Shanco who was by the fire, so that he could make the mash. She listened to Jack and Judy's smalltalk as she mixed in the flour.

'Have you been married, Judy?'

Martha's words fell across them like an axe. Jack shifted his weight from one buttock to the other.

'Not so's you'd notice, Maa-tha.'

The way she said her name made Martha blush.

'But you've got children, though?'

'Yeh, two.'

'And where is their father?'

There was silence except the sound of Martha's gravy-spoon and Shanco's mashing.

'Well, one's in Leeds, like, where I left 'im, and one's i'n't army.'

'I see.'

Jack's face was bright red. Martha brought the food to the table.

'Looks great! Not been too much bother for you, eh?'

'No, not on your account, anyway. It's our mother's birthday today and we celebrate it every year.'

'Oh, she must be knockin' on a bit by now; how old?'

'She's dead – help yourself.'

Shanco came over for once and sat by Martha. She noticed Jack had scrubbed his nails clean.

'Jack's been right kind to me, you know.'

Martha raised her eyebrows.

'Said it'd be OK to keep me 'orses here if I want, like. So sweet, 'e is! That's where we met, like. Me buying feed at the…'

'We don't like horses,' Martha said. 'They contribute nothing to the farm.'

Jack spoke in Welsh to Martha, 'Just like you then.' Martha stopped eating with a quick response in kind, 'Shut up, Jack. You know it's Mami's birthday and if she can't show a little respect I'm sure you can have a go.'

'Well, Mami was a lot of help, wasn't she? If she'd done the right thing then none of us would be stuck here up shit-creek.'

'Maybe she'd her own reasons for not leaving this place to you, Jack. Looking at you and Lady Muck here I'd say she had a very good reason.'

18

Judy couldn't understand but was trying to ignore it all anyway by tucking into her meal. Martha got up and started tidying the kitchen. The others ate in silence. She came back to clear the plates and then fetched a blackberry tart from the dresser, putting it in the middle of the table.

'Tart?' she asked Judy, enjoying the innuendo. She cut the pieces before Judy had the chance to answer and she watched the dark juice bleeding through the golden crust. She put milk on the table for the tart and sat down quietly.

After tea Judy and Jack went to sit in the parlour and all you could hear was bursts of Judy's girlish laughter. Shanco listened but his mind was elsewhere.

The dishes cleared, Martha went to the door to put on her wellingtons. She took her overcoat and walked out. It was a crisp clear night and the moon was nearly full. She walked over the yard and up to the storehouse. Up the steps and she sat at the top.

From here you could see right up and down the valley. She watched the village lights spread their orange mist down in the valley but on the far hill the darkness was complete. She always wondered how Graig-ddu looked from up there. It was just as black there. Was Gwynfor out in that darkness?

You could see the church from here too. That had been on the farmland originally. Tonight it looked silver with the moonlight catching the graves now and then to make Christmas lights. All the Graig-ddu family had been buried there; instead of being in the middle of the plot, the family graves kept as close to the farm boundary as possible. Well isn't that odd, thought Martha. Each one looking down over the farm and keeping an eye on it. She shivered, partly because of what she was thinking and partly because of the cold. She heard footsteps. Shanco was hanging about. He

19

climbed up too to sit by her. Bob was sleeping soundly under his coat. Both of them sat quietly.

'Our f... f.. family got planted here didn't we, Martha?'

She smiled. 'You're right, love, Shanco.'

'When will they come up?'

'Can't say, Shanco; Springtime, maybe.'

The two of them heard a door closing and footsteps on the yard. Then a car starting up. Both followed the car lights all the way up the lane until pitch black folded around them once more.

SIX

Thursday morning Martha was getting ready for town. She'd ironed her blue suit already. Every Thursday was the same. Down to town in Jack's old car, fetch Shanco's pills and Jack's pension, to the Co-op to get food, do the errands and then call in the café before coming home to make tea. She leaned forward and looked through her bedroom window to see if she needed her heavy coat.

There in the yard, Shanco was skulking about. She watched him briefly. He looked around him then walked between the tractor and the trailer. When he was out of sight, she noticed the window needed cleaning. He appeared again almost straight away and he was running for his life. He hid behind the wall of the milking parlour. Martha knew what would happen next and she settled back to enjoy the show. Jack appeared with a curl of cigarette smoke around his head. He was striding about the place as usual. He pulled himself up into the tractor cab and closed the door. He turned the ignition on and released the handbrake. Shanco sank lower behind the wall. She was already smiling. Jack put the tractor in gear and off he went, but the trailer stayed behind in the middle of the yard. By the time Jack's curses reached the yard, Shanco was well away into the haybarn with the lynchpin safe in his pocket.

Martha laughed again before dabbing a bit more powder on her nose and choosing a necklace. She looked at the golden pile snaking over the table. She chose one that

Gwynfor had given her but put it back and wore her mother's instead. She clicked off the bakelite switch and went out. Jack was out in the yard.

'Martha! Seen that lad?' Shanco's mischief had lit his fuse.

'No, Jack.'

'And where're you off to then? It's always me's got to do the lot here, isn't it?'

She threw her bag on the passenger seat.

'To town. If you want tea tonight, I've got to go fetch a few things. Something to say about that then, have you?'

Jack hesitated, then lowered his head. He turned and wandered over to the dog sheds. As Martha faced the car towards the yard gate she saw Jack take hold of Bob by his back legs and hold him upside down over the cows' water trough.

'Shanco!' Jack shouted at the top of his voice.

'If you don't bring that fucking pin back here right now then little Bobi's going to get his first swimming lesson!' His smile was pure malice.

She watched the little dog squirming like a fish on the hook. As she drove up the lane she looked back to see Shanco blundering out, his eyes big with fear.

Town was busy and she took longer than usual getting things done. It was market day too and Eurwen's café was packed. Martha ordered a cup of milky coffee and a cake. She always drank coffee here; she could have tea at home. She'd go for something a bit exotic, not the everyday scones and pancakes. She sat down and waited for one of the girls to bring what she'd ordered to the table. She never talked to anyone in the café, just sat listening and noticing what the other women were wearing.

The café hadn't changed much over the years. The wooden counter was just the same, and the blue sign above it with the same old words: Cigarettes, Sweets and Minerals. The red formica tabletops had worn in white clouds where elbows leaned; salt spilt over them would jump when the plates came banging down. She always had to fight back the temptation to go fetch a cloth and wipe them clean. It was the same with the mirror, a huge thing filling one wall, put there by a far-sighted owner to pretend the place was double its size.

The biggest change was the girls behind the counter. These were younger and ruder. Not like the waitresses that first time Martha met Gwynfor there on a market day. Now you had to swallow up your coffee and cake quick to make room for someone else. Taking tea out had been a leisurely affair when she'd go there with Mami in the old days. It was cleaner then too, she thought. She realised the café had emptied and she heard the impatient tapping of nails on the counter. She placed the right change on the table and left.

As she came into the yard, she saw a stranger's car. Walking towards the door after collecting her things, she wondered which rep had called by. It was too early for the cake rep and the man selling the milking parlour cleaning stuff had already been. She noticed there was steam on the kitchen windows. She pushed open the door, struggling with the weight of the Co-op bags. She let the bags fall to the floor, apples rolling everywhere. Shanco watched them until one apple slowed down, trembled and stopped at Judy's feet.

'Oh dea',' Judy smiled, making no effort to pick it up. 'Hope you don' mind duck,' she went on, 'but I've made't tea already, seeing's you're soh late. Spag Bol. You can freeze tha' stuff you got there, yeh?'

23

SEVEN

'Mmmartha, Martha.'

She felt someone pulling on the bedclothes. She woke to look up into Shanco's pale face. He was standing in his long johns, jumping in the cold from one foot to the other. He was terribly thin.

'C... c... can't sleep.'

Martha sat up and turned back the blankets. She took the feather bolster from under the pillows and turned it, then put it down the middle of the bed to divide it. She moved over to the other half of the bed. The pillow and the blanket were cold on that side. He got in the other side, his weight making Martha bounce a second.

This had been happening for weeks, despite her hoping he had got used to sleeping on his own by now.

Jack and Judy had put up a tent in Cae Marged. Judy insisted they sleep in it when her children were home. When the weather was cold or the children were with their father, they'd stay in her council house in Dewi Crescent. Martha couldn't believe it when she first saw the tent. Jack and Shanco had slept together since they were tots, and since there were only three bedrooms at Graig-ddu and one of those full of Mami's things, that had suited everybody.

Martha just couldn't get to sleep. She smiled sadly – because Jack wasn't there, Shanco couldn't sleep and so he came to Martha's bed, while Martha couldn't sleep because she couldn't get used to sharing. Shanco had nodded off now and she sat up again, listening to his heavy breathing. She sometimes wished she could be like him, sleeping like a baby.

From her bed Martha could see through the deepset window out to the yard and the fields above. It was a cold night tonight. Jack and Judy would definitely be in her council house.

Soon they'd have to think about Christmas, she thought. Two turkeys were in the shed, eating up in happy ignorance. It was Shanco's job to feed them and for some of their meals he would sit watching them. They kept an extra in case something happened to either of them. If both survived they'd eat one at Easter. One year both their heads turned black. They looked awful and it was Mami said a spider should be put down their gullets or they wouldn't get any better. Shanco was the one to do it of course, even though he was scared silly of spiders. He had to go to the old red cowshed and throw water along the old mud wall. You could get huge spiders there, and he spent all day trying to catch them and blubbering like a baby when he did. Mami said they had to go down their throats head first or the medicine wouldn't work. Jack had done the milking and fed the cows by the time Shanco came out of that shed all sweat and feathers. But it did the trick: the turkeys got better.

They'd have to go down the valley to look for holly and ivy. Shanco moved at her side and let out a long noisy fart. Martha looked at him. At least he was keeping still tonight. Sometimes he'd be tossing and turning as though his demons were up and prodding him from within. He would pull the most awful faces, scaring Martha, until she reminded herself it was only Shanco after all. Tonight his face was even and distant, his white bristles making him look somehow younger. She felt his forehead. His face was cold. She noticed his square chin, his hollow cheeks, his skin stretched tight across his skull like poor pasture skimming the hilltop. Under his chin was a scab from shaving, surrounded by a ring of blood and around that a circle of dark whiskers where he'd left off shaving there some days back.

Keeping her hand on his forehead, Martha wondered where Gwynfor was tonight. Friday night had become the same as any other. His visits used to make a marker on the week, around which she could get things organised. Say on a Monday, she might come across something in the paper and tell herself to mention it to him. Or she might try a new cake recipe and look forward to Friday's adjudication. Every day was the same now. She imagined Jack and Judy curled up together in her council house.

She looked again through the window and saw the bats playing like fish. And then came the cat, moving like quicksilver, her time of mourning long gone. Martha watched her move smooth as butter. Then, seeing something, she stopped, ready to pounce. The cloud shifted briefly, revealing the moon's full brightness for an instant, catching the green canvas tent in its spotlight, a blister on the field's green skin.

EIGHT

The turkeys were killed first thing. The rain was a sheet and the yard a muddy puddle. The water ran through the milking yard, settling in pools in the dung heap at the bottom of the yard. Bits of straw spun on the water's surface. It was grey and miserable, the only proper light coming from the red cowshed where Jack and Martha were trying to catch the turkeys with Shanco and Bob watching them from the stalls.

'Watch out, woman! Hold it there now; close that door!'

'Jack, behind you!'

The turkey jumped at Jack, knocking him against the wall.

'Jack, we'd better let them settle down a bit,' Martha shouted over the babble.

'What?'

'We'd better have a bit of a break so they calm down!' She shouted louder this time.

'We'll get the buggers now! Come round here, Martha!'

Jack was trying to pen in both turkeys using an old door, so that she could take a proper hold of one of them. But the turkeys seemed to have an idea of what was in store for them and they weren't giving in easily. It would have been easier if he had scraped down the cowshed before the job started; the floor was thick with old hard dung that was awfully dangerous to walk on.

'Jesus, woman, what's wrong with you? Catch the fuckers or we'll be here till New Year!'

Every time Martha went for one of their necks, either the

door, or Jack or the wall would get in the way; if she managed to get hold of one properly, the brute would fight like a tiger. Twenty-nine pounds of angry turkey is not a feather pillow; they can snap your arm like a twig.

In a little while she was tiring and the turkeys' wings were beating up dust, bringing tears to her eyes and making it even harder to catch them. He was swearing in buckets and every now and again he'd kick the door he was using. His face was bright red. He decided to change tack so he dumped the door and started to wave his arms like a windmill instead.

Martha heard a noise above that of the turkeys, the rain and Jack's shouting. A noise from the far end of the cowshed. It was Shanco doubled up laughing and pointing at Jack. Martha looked at him too and saw the joke. Jack carried on waving his arms, not knowing the others were looking at him. His belly was bouncing up and down, and his neck was the colour of bacon. He looked just as wild as the turkeys.

Martha started laughing too until she felt ill and had to lean against the wall. Both of them were laughing together as they used to when they were children. Bob wasn't used to how Shanco's belly was shaking and he joined them, howling. This only made Martha and Shanco laugh louder and in the end, his arms still waving, Jack came to see what was so funny. He stared at them a minute in silence then barked, 'Come on, that's enough cackling! Do something, for God's sake!'

But as he turned to pick up the door again a smile played around his lips, and even Jack couldn't hide it.

To make it easier to pluck them, they hung the turkeys on the old milking machine. After about four minutes, most of the feathers had come off, and the three used pliers to tackle the most awkward ones on the wings. They were working quietly with Bob snuffling in the cow mess, his nose red from turkey blood. It was like snow in the cowshed; now and then Shanco would blow the falling feathers from his brow. In about a quarter of an hour the floor was quite white. When they'd finished they wrapped both bodies in blankets to keep them warm, and carried them like hot water bottles through the rain to the house. Martha had made sandwiches that morning to save time. The little table had been put out ready for the two parcels.

Jack went to the stove to make tea. He poured the water into the teapot; as usual he took off his hat, put it on the teapot and carried it to the table. A day's plucking was one of those rare occasions when he would fill the teapot. He went to the door and took off his shoes so that he could sit by the fire. He was looking for his tobacco. Shanco was sitting by his side, his eyes half-closing and Bob on his belly shivering like barbed wire someone's given a twang.

Martha cut off the heads and the feet first and threw them in the bucket under the little table. She cut the throats, getting out the meat and putting it aside for soup. She drew out the stomach and the windpipe, putting the tube on the table too, ready for the performance to follow. Then she cut a notch in both tail-ends and pulled out the intestines, carefully removing the bile sac next to the liver without breaking it. She opened both gizzards too so that Shanco could see what was in them. One year they'd found a little button and he'd kept that for luck. These were a cock and a hen anyway, and Martha looked at the small wet, bright eggs like fish eggs in the hen's womb.

She washed the turkeys and took them out of the way to

the pantry, coming back to wash her hands. She took her tea and sandwich then sat down, Jack and Shanco watching her in silence.

'Weather's a bitch,' Jack said, to himself rather than anyone in particular. 'It's never like this at Christmas. Damn dirty rain.'

In response the rain rapped louder on the windows as though it wanted a welcome and a place by the fire. Gusts were blowing from under the outer door, lifting the wallpaper around the windows. The fire flared up.

'Fuckin' Christmas, my God....'

When she'd finished her tea she fetched the windpipe from the little table and Shanco brightened. She straightened the wet pink tube and blew into it a tune something like *Jingle Bells*. Shanco was creasing up laughing, and even Jack was smiling.

Every year Martha would play the windpipe, Shanco would laugh and Jack would smile. Christmas was coming.

NINE

Martha was steaming out sweat, the heat from the stove searing her eyes each time she opened the oven. She'd had to cut off the turkey's legs to get it in the oven and as she'd taken it out, the hot fat had spilled on the lino, making it slippery. She started clearing the plates after dinner.

'Thanks,' Jack said, leaning back on the settle and rubbing his sides. He was sitting with his collar open, and his flies too, to make room for his belly. Shanco was already sleeping by the fire, a red party hat on his head. Bob was sniffing out scraps under the table. For the dog it was a feast day too, and a chance for a fine dinner.

'Good stuff this, too,' Jack grabbed the square bottle of fast-disappearing whisky, 'this old Jack... Jack Daniels.' He poured himself another measure. 'Let's have some of that Corona pop.'

They could hear a car in the yard. Martha's shoulders stiffened at the sink. Shanco woke up with a start at Bob's barking. She looked at Jack but he wouldn't look back at her. Judy came in all smiles, wearing Christmassy tinsel earrings, and she sat down next to Jack. Jack poured her a shot of whisky.

Ugh, thought Martha, a woman drinking like that on Christmas Day.

Judy watched her clearing up without saying anything; just threw a smile her way now and then like a knife-thrower at the circus. Each smile close to cutting flesh. Shanco went back to sleep, the spark of interest on her arrival snuffed out.

'And where are your children today then, Judy?' Martha asked in English.

She glanced at her in surprise then looked her in the eye.

'Brian picked 'em up this aft. If you'd got kids yeh'd know you gorra get away from 'em too,' she said. Talking to Judy was like walking through a nettle field. Jack was pouring another glass. 'Reckon theh'd like it 'ere though; always liked the countryside, them.'

Martha carried on washing up, ignoring her. Whenever Judy came she felt cold hands at her throat; pressing harder every visit. Scouring the roasting tin she thought of Gwynfor. She scrubbed it harder and left it clean.

Jack was telling another story. She went to the dresser; feeling invisible she poured herself some ginger beer and sat down. Bob came out from under the table and jumped into her lap.

He always liked to tell a story, but he was in fine form tonight what with the whisky and a new member in the audience. The first one was about that time he went shooting crows in the valley. The crows were bigger when he was younger, so he said, so's it was dangerous to shoot in case one fell on his head. Jack only told these stories when he was tanked up, and his face lit up when he described in English for Judy how he'd shot three crows.

'They were so big, – *this* big,' he said holding out his arms, 'I could only fit three in the back of the Land Rover.'

Judy laughed a bit too loudly and a bit too long. Bob looked up at her in surprise. Judy noticed it.

'Oh, stop tha' thing looking at me, will you Jack?'

She looked towards Martha. Jack looked reluctantly over

32

to the dog in Martha's lap and grabbed one of his shoes, throwing it at the dog. Since he was drunk, he missed and the shoe landed heavily on Martha's belly. Jack and Judy looked at each other and burst out laughing. Martha felt bruised and Bob attacked the shoe on the floor, gnawing it wildly while he looked up sympathetically at Martha. No word of apology from Jack.

'The fields are that big in America, you see, they plough up them one day and they come back the next!'

The laughter died down after a while and Judy noticed Martha looking towards them. She took her hand from Jack's and stretched it out to Martha.

'And wha' d'you think of this eh, Maatha? Inni' luvly?'

Martha got up and went over to her. Her hands were red and swollen from all the hot water. She took Judy's hand and saw a gold ring on her finger. First thing she noticed was it wasn't on her wedding finger. Second, she recognised the ring. It was Mami's. Martha felt all weak and her temper rose in a wave.

'It's ma Christmas pressie,' Judy looked at Jack, smiling. He didn't know what to say but he stammered, 'But I said – we said – it was going to be a secret!'

'Woops, forgot; sorreh,' Judy smiled at Martha.

Martha turned to Jack in Welsh. 'You can't do it, Jack. You had no right.'

At least Jack answered in her own language, 'Oh don't start on me again,' but he let her go on.

'You can't do it. You've no right to give it away.' Her voice was rising dangerously.

'I'm the oldest so I should've had everything. It'd've been mine then, no question.'

'But it *wasn't* yours, Jack, and you had no right.'

'Well it's time one of us started things moving here... nothing ever changes.... No one owns anything here, do they? And where's that man of yours today then? That's why you're in a bad mood, is it? At least I've got 'er 'ere with me today.'

All those words Martha wanted to say right now were blocked in her throat. Her eyes had the same expression as that cat miaowing up on the top rafters in the haybarn the day Bob killed the kittens.

'Wake up will you, Jack,' she said quietly.

She walked over to the door and put her coat on.

'Where're you going?' Jack asked her, Martha's words having sobered him up.

'M... M... Martha,' Shanco began.

'You shut your mouth too. Get out will you,' Jack's other shoe flew at Shanco and he disappeared upstairs with his tail between his legs. Judy snaked her arm back around Jack's.

Martha answered Jack, 'To put a wreath on Mami's grave, like I do every year.'

She took the plastic bag from the dresser and shut the door firmly behind her.

TEN

She usually welcomed the cold on her face but tonight the mist chafed her cheeks. Night was drawing in and her eyes took a while to get used to the dark. The cattle were gathering in the yard ready for milking, Christmas Day like any other. Martha's hands carrying the bag were getting chilled, and she pulled her collar tighter.

Every year she would walk up the lane to the top then through the fields and over the hedge into the cemetery to put a wreath on Mami's grave. Usually this would be a fine walk following festive overeating and the walking would give her time to think. She would think of all the other Christmas Days she had spent in Graig-ddu. Of the New Year and of other things she kept buried inside the rest of the year. That was odd, she thought, almost stumbling over a stone. How people buried thoughts only to resurrect them now and then to persuade themselves they had been alive.

Tonight the thoughts were like a thousand balloons in her head, each slyly trying to edge the other out of its way. It was so hard to concentrate on just one thing. She reached the end of the lane and looked back at the house. It all took her right back to when she was a little girl; the scene the same except for the shiny-backed cars like beetles spoiling the yard.

She gripped the bag tighter and decided to climb the gate instead of opening it. She used to get a row from Dat for doing that when she was little. As if the weight of a little girl would break the hinges. She smiled. Dat had beaten Mami to the grave by over twenty years. Mami was always cursing him for leaving her on her own. Martha could still somehow hear his lungs rasping. Tonight she didn't mind about damaging the gate so she lifted her leg awkwardly over it, taking care not to ladder her tights. She landed on the other side with a scrunch. She looked at the church. The Christmas services finished at four so it was pretty likely no one would be about.

Closely, like a fox, she followed the hedge up to the church wall. She looked over it to check no one was there. She pulled herself over the hedge, using the trunk of a strong hawthorn. Mami's voice came to her as though she was there with her:

When you see a hawthorn bright,
Her curls a crown, frothing white,
At her root the green shoot's quick
Now's the time the seeds will take.

Her tights caught in the thorns as she pushed past, drawing blood. The grass was short in the graveyard, the earth hard as gunshot. She had fallen just short of the family's graves. She looked at them, lined up smart as sailors, the black marble engraved in gold. It was ship-shape: Mami would've been so proud. She put her hand on Mami and Dat's grave. The marble was as cold and smooth as Shanco's forehead that night in bed. She stood a while looking down on Graig-ddu. The breeze was shifting a long dark smear of firesmoke in the sky. The light was still on in Shanco's room. Martha imagined him sitting on his bed, still in the paper hat, listening to Jack and Judy's laughter from the parlour. She looked behind her at the rows of graves. The scene was like a Christmas card with its yew trees weeping quietly each side of the walk picking its way from the church door to the little gate.

She took the wreath out of the bag and placed it on Mami and Dat's grave. There were never any flowers except her flowers on the graves: the three of them were the only family left. She looked at the moss circle licked by its red curl of ribbon. It had holly on it too. She had to buy holly each year, since the two holly trees in the garden were barren of berries. She guessed the trees must be sisters or brothers. No future flush of baby red berries, then. From its black stone, the wreath's eye was fixed on Martha, making her blush. Putting her hand to her lips she pressed the kiss into the gravestone and turned to climb back into the field. She followed the hedges but this time turned left in the second field across the lane and into Cae Marged. She walked fast, her breath ghosting the air. She looked fearfully around her though no one ever followed her. Her hands were getting cold. She went to the field's top hedge and stood under the bare branches of the big oak which reached far above. She stood there for a second. She took hold of the fence and carried on looking around. She opened the plastic bag and pulled another wreath out of it. She carefully sat down at the foot of the hedge and pulled up her legs towards her chest like a little girl. Her eyes were dark and wet in the moonlight; her hair was bright. On the other side of the field stood the tent. The wind had pulled one corner down and it was gaping open.

Martha started to cry. Crying like the end of the world. She cried until her eyes were red and her face sopping. She cried until her nose ran and she could hear her own blood

37

beating in her head. Her sobbing wasn't pretty. There was no stopping the sound of it, like that of a fox howling. She gripped the wobbly circle of the wreath of flowers as though it were a life buoy. *When you see a hawthorn bright, her curls a crown, frothing white*. Then her breath started to steady. She dried her face with a hanky and used the fence to help her get up slowly. She pushed the wreath into the dark of the hedge's tangle. This one had no ribbon, had nothing that would show up after the rest had rotted away. It looked like a little nest in the undergrowth.

Like a little nest for the Spring. *Now's the time the seeds will take*. No good came of anything sown before then since the earth was too cold and unready. Martha wound up the plastic bag and pushed it into her pocket; then she walked slowly homeward.

Behind the bottom hedge Shanco got up. He'd been in a quandary: should he go and comfort his sister or not? If he had done, she'd have known he'd sneaked out of the house. Every year Shanco faced the same dilemma as he followed her up to the church and watched her from a distance. Hidden behind the hedge he would listen to the weeping with his stomach knotted. Every year he'd never pluck up the nerve to go to her, and every year he would run home before she got there. He ran quietly back to the house, his woolly hat pulled tight over his red paper crown.

ELEVEN

It was hard getting the paper to light. Martha splashed onto the fire some more of the red diesel from the Lucozade bottle in her hand. The lawn under the fire was wet and so the flames were slow to catch. The air filled with black smoke which caught the back of her throat.

'Come on, Shanco love. Bring everything out so we can get rid of some of this mess.'

Shanco's head was hidden behind a pile of cardboard boxes.

'Ugh, there's always so much rubbish left behind after Christmas,' Martha whispered.

The flames leapt higher as he threw on more waste paper from the house. Both of them stood watching the fire. The edges of the paper curled slowly and the sheets were black as a crow's wings. Black smuts were in the air like black snow. Some of them fell on Shanco's face, blackening his cheeks when he rubbed them. Jack appeared.

'What you doin'?'

He went back to the house to fetch another load.

'Clearing up a bit around here. We've really got to get rid of these. How can I keep the house tidy with all this rubbish lying around?'

'Well it'll rain soon and it'll all get damp. Then we'll 'ave all this crap at the bottom of the garden for ages.'

Jack stooped to light his fag from the flames. He stayed like that for a while, looking deep into the fire. He didn't stand up straight away, partly because he was enjoying the warmth on his face, and partly because his back was aching.

'What you got 'ere anyway?'

'Just some old stuff.'

'Nothin' important I 'ope.'

'Well if you're worried about some old will, Jack, you won't find that in there.' He looked at her, surprised. 'And talking of rubbish, is she coming over again tonight then?'

'Oh shut up, will you? You're always bangin' on about her.'

'Just asking.'

He got up slowly, taking a drag on his cigarette.

'Well, if you asked a bit more about Gwynfor and a bit less about Judy, you'd be on the right track.'

'What d'you mean?'

''Eard he's seein' someone else, that's all. Just someone, you know, quite a bit younger.'

She looked at the fire. She was glad she was already flushed from the heat of the flames. Jack studied her face.

'You'll lose your chance there, Martha. Must be loads o' women after 'im. I'm tellin' you, there's only so much people can put up with.' His face was like an envelope, opening. She watched the red light of the flames on his face. 'There's nothin' 'ere, Martha. It's all finished. We're all finished.'

'Don't talk like that, Jack. You don't know everything, you know,' she whispered, taking a stick to push some paper back into the middle of the fire.

'What's there to know? I'll tell you: you don't 'ave to stay here any longer. You can go.'

'So you get to keep the lot then, Jack, is it? After all these years of working, traipsing through that mud. That's all I get then, is it? "Goodbye"?' Their faces were inches away from each other. There was no stopping Martha now. 'Just for you to get the lot and move those scroungers in to spend all Mami and Dat's money, is it? I tell you, every single one of our family lying out there in that graveyard has sweated blood! They've bent over backwards to give us what we've got today, and that's how you're going to spend it, is it?'

Her hands were shaking as she held the stick. Jack had let his fag fall to the ground.

'Martha, listen, will you? If Mami'd given me the lot, like she should 'ave, you'd've been free to leave anyway.' Mami had broken with tradition by not leaving the farm to her eldest son, and Jack had felt the slight ever since.

'But she didn't do that, did she? And what about Shanco? You never think about him, do you?'

'Martha, come on, he's not all there!' Jack shouted, jabbing the side of his head with his finger. She looked at him and he calmed down as he looked back into the flames. 'You know how Shanco is,' he went on, 'he's been a millstone around my neck all these years.' Both listened to the paper burning. 'That old bitch screwed us up good and proper.'

'Don't ever...'

'She tied us hand and foot to this place, Martha. She knew just what she was doin'! Dat must've turned in his grave.'

'I'm surprised you even remember they're dead! You never talk about them!'

'What for? What d'you want me to say? What d'you want me to do? Go and kneel over their graves? Pretend I'm mournin' for the old sods?'

Martha wasn't listening.

'Mami knew what she was doing,' she reasoned, 'she was

making sure whichever one of us puts the most in, will get to keep the lot.'

'The stupidest, more like. Whichever one of us is stupid enough to work like a dog 'til it's all over.'

'Well why don't you go then, Jack?'

'And why don' you go then, Martha?'

The two looked at each other with the smoke all around them. Jack's hands were shaking and his heart pounding painfully in his chest. It was hard to breathe. The smoke was burning his lungs and his heart was hurting again from that old pain.

'You've got a chance, Martha. Get out of here. It's too late for me. I can't get what you can.'

'And what is that, Jack?'

The wind fanned the flames red. They'd climbed high by now with blazing bright scraps flying into the trees around the garden. The branches were thin like veins in an afterbirth. She noticed Jack was short of breath.

'I know somethin's keeping you here, Martha, I do know that.'

She looked into his eyes. She wasn't sure but his face seemed softer, his eyes deeper. She looked at him for quite a while. Maybe it was the firelight doing that to his face, maybe the smoke was softening the light.

'I don't know what you're talking about, Jack,' Martha said, concentrating on the stick in her hand.

'You *do* know, Matty.'

The girlhood nickname brought all her defences down for a second. She stopped moving and stayed as though frozen in the fire's heat. Her eyes were darting back and forth between Jack and the fire.

'You won't get rid of me as easy as that, Jack Williams.'

42

The heat was by now too much for him and he looked at her wildly.

'That's it then Martha, you 'ad your chance and you've blown it. Just don't expect an easy ride around here from now on.'

Jack spat into the fire, any tenderness gone from his face. His eyes hardened again. She threw the stick right into the flames. Jack limped away. Martha saw that Shanco had been watching from behind the rhododendron bush, the black snow falling around him. A pile of boxes was scattered at his feet and the tears had made furrows down the soot on his face. She looked at him and listened to the tap-tap of the stick burning slowly. It started to rain.

TWELVE

'M... *Martha*! M... Martha!'

Shanco ran around the corner so fast he had to grab the edge of the shed to stop himself skidding headlong. Bob came after him, his white paws all muddy. She was in the big shed getting the pens ready for lambing.

'Come on!'

The smile on his face told the whole story. Martha tied the last gate to the one next to it and walked out of the shed. Her footsteps were followed by six black noses under the dog sheds as she went across the yard. She reached the bottom of the garden. The two of them walked through the ash of yesterday's fire and there in the hedge the little light green spears of snowdrops were slicing through the earth. Shanco was smiling and pointing at the same time. They were a fine little cluster too, and she knew he would come down every day to see them until they were in flower. He'd watch out for bluebells in May as well, and when there was a little white head among the blue ones he'd go even dafter. She stooped to pull away last year's long grass around them, giving it to him to throw away. The grass was old, yellow and coarse.

'J... J... Judy's hair!' Shanco exclaimed, putting it on his head and looking at Martha. She realised that this was the first time he had said Judy's name. She began to laugh.

'What's so funny?' The voice startled them both. She got up and dried her hands in her apron.

'Gwynfor! We didn't hear you coming.'

'Sorry.'

'No, don't worry.' He looked at her. 'Would you like some tea?'

'No thank you, I've come to talk to you.'

Shanco gave him a long look because he had interrupted him and his sister laughing.

Gwynfor was wearing a new dark blue suit but on its knees there were two big pawprints where Roy had greeted him. There were also signs that a comb had recently ploughed his hair. He gave Shanco a sheepish smile and he smiled back. Gwynfor's smile widened and he raised his eyebrows at Shanco. Back came Shanco's smile, as wide as a church door this time, and he raised his own eyebrows. Gwynfor shifted his weight from one leg to the other. Martha eventually decided to help him.

'Shanco, go and light the fire, will you? The kindling at the bottom of the stove is dry already.' She didn't usually let him light the fire so she expected him to jump at the chance but today he wasn't even nibbling at the bait. 'Shanco, go and light the fire!'

'N... n... no!' He drew himself up to his full height. He was over six feet tall but as slight as a rush. Martha looked at him in surprise. Gwynfor laughed quietly.

'Wh... wh... wh,' Shanco stuttered like an old tractor engine.

'Shanco, go and light the fire now!' She stood before him.

'Shanco, you'd be a big help to Martha if you went to light the fire, and if you do I'll bring you more sweets from town next week.'

You could almost see Shanco's obstinacy escaping. The puff went out of his chest and his shoulders sank. He looked from

45

Martha to Gwynfor in confusion until she nodded towards the house. Then he ran as fast as he could to do his task.

'D'you want to come to the parlour?' she asked. 'It's wet here.' She noticed his shoes were dirty from standing on the wet earth.

'Martha, you know why I'm here.'

'Do we have to discuss it out here?'

'Yes, and that's final.' There was a new decisiveness in Gwynfor's eyes. Martha felt the blood rushing to her head. 'There's room for you at Troed-rhiw. We'll get married and we'd be company for each other. You know I think the world of you.' He paused and looked at her. 'And another thing, I've bought you a piano. It's in the parlour at Troed-rhiw. They brought it yesterday and it's a fine one too – the best in the shop – and it came with books and all the stuff you'll need to learn it.'

She felt the strangest pressure in her stomach as though all the snowdrops' spears were spiking through her belly.

'I know this place is important to you. After twenty years, I know that, you've got to believe me. I've been thinking, and I'm happy for Shanco to come too, even after today's performance. He can have his own room and he can help me around the yard. He's a handy lad to fetch things and he could be a big help to me. He'd be doing me a favour, to be honest.'

He looked tired and his hands were wringing his cloth cap.

'Well what do you say? Yes or no?'

Martha's eyes wouldn't stay still. Her thoughts were running all ways like water. She saw that Jack was standing in the yard smoking. He was leaning against Gwynfor's car and watching them. He lifted his head for a moment and looked towards her. There was something about the way he was standing. A shudder went through her.

46

'Has Jack got something to do with this?' Martha asked.

'What?'

'Has Jack been talking to you?'

'What d'you mean, talking to me?'

Look, I'm not stupid,' she said. 'He wants to get me out of here. He's just about itching to get rid of me. It's no secret we've been like cats and dogs lately. It's a fair enough question. Has he been talking to you or not? Has he offered you something maybe?'

Her voice was shaking and she was too scared to stop talking in case she started crying then and there.

Gwynfor looked at her, deep down hurt showing in his eyes. She felt something break. He had put his cap back on his head.

'It's obvious,' he said, 'you don't know me at all. I can't forgive you for suggesting such a thing.'

Gwynfor turned on his heel and Martha watched him go. She saw Jack going towards him and trying to find out what had happened. Gwynfor pushed past him, went into his car and left.

'Fuckin' hell!' Jack said, shaking his head as he took his shepherd's crook and went towards the dog sheds. Martha made her way towards the house so that she could get the tea on. Her head was low and she noticed Gwynfor's footprints in the mud. She looked at them. Perfect footprints. Even the size and the tread were clearly stamped there. She fetched an old washing up bowl from the garden wall and placed it over the prints. Her stomach felt as though she had been salted like pork; she had no tears left because they'd all dried up inside. She went into the house and saw Shanco still searching for the kindling at the bottom of the stove.

THIRTEEN

Will Tyddyn Gwyn brought the plough over first thing. Through the window Martha watched him and Jack talking in the yard. Both were lost in a cloud of tobacco smoke. Will was a short man; age had folded him almost in half, like a book. He wore a cloth cap askew; when he wanted to pick up speed, he would turn it right round so that the peak faced backwards and then carry on at just the same pace. He always had on a waistcoat, shirt and tie even though he lived on his own and never saw anyone from week to week. He wore mustard-coloured shoes. Mami always said that any man who wore shoes on a farm instead of wellingtons must be a bit of a dandy. Martha remembered Will in primary school. He'd come over after school and the four of them would go and play in the haybarn or down in the woods. She was always the one to get left at the bottom of the tree holding Shanco's hand, while the others climbed way up above. After Will left school to stay at home so that he could work for his mother, Martha hardly ever saw him.

His mother was a strong woman in a blue woollen cardigan and flowery apron; she had a tin of mints on the mantelshelf ready for any children who called round. Martha remembered getting one of these once. The sweet had been there so long it was soft. Jack always said those mints were older than he was! She kept a pet duck too, a little black feather boat waddling over the lino and shitting everywhere.

Martha saw Jack getting packets of tobacco out of his

pocket and pushing them towards Will. He accepted this offering and pushed them deep into his pocket, nodding. This was the annual payment for borrowing the plough. There wasn't enough work at Graig-ddu to justify buying one. The deal hadn't yet been clinched, though. She wrapped the cakes in a cloth and put them in a cardboard box. She walked towards the men. Will nodded to her without saying a word. She opened the door of his tractor and placed the box inside by the seat. The door banged shut. Will nodded once again and watched her return to the house. Jack broke his reverie.

'When you counted your sheep the other day, did you see them three pet lambs that escaped from the small field last year?'

Will shook his head.

'Now then,' he said slowly, on his guard, 'let me think.'

Talking to Will was like peeling an onion. You had to get under several layers of skin before reaching his heart.

'I know they went over there,' Jack said, giving him another chance to confess.

'Maybe they have, maybe they have,' he answered, rocking to and fro on his heels.

'Strong ones, in good condition. Shanco'd been feedin' them for months. Milk that doesn't end up in the tank's a waste of money.'

Will felt the fine fullness of his pocket where he'd stuffed his Golden Virginia. He thought of the fruit cakes in the tractor. Maybe there'd be scones there, or a tart, or drop scones. Since his mother died he'd had to eat cheap shop-bought cakes.

'Just don't understand,' Jack went on, 'don't understand where they went if it wasn't over your way.'

Will took another drag on his cigarette. He blew the smoke slowly out through his nostrils. He threw the stub to the ground and squashed it deliberately with his right foot.

'You know what they say, Jack.' Will had a way of pausing; he moved closer to Jack's ear and said in English, 'Good fences make good neighbours.'

Jack could feel his temper rising but he knew he'd have to borrow Will's bailer in the summer so he stifled it.

Will turned towards the tractor and climbed the steep steps up to the cab. Since tractors had got so big and Will had shrunk with age, he'd welded an extra step under the proper one to make it easier to climb in. Will was one for an easy life. He started up the tractor and the plough came down onto the yard. Jack disconnected the tractor from the plough. Will drove away without looking back.

Today Martha would have to take a snack to the field for Jack, so she started opening a tin and mashed the salmon with vinegar to soften it. There were cakes left over after filling Will's box, the ones that had burnt a little from being at the back of the oven. It wouldn't do to offer those to a visitor. She wrapped them with the sandwiches and put them on the table. Before Will arrived, Jack had been up in Cae Marged, taking the tent down and relocating it right in the corner, out of the way of the plough. Shanco had been watching the whole business with shining eyes. Lately he'd started going to look at the tent every now and then, and Martha'd had to warn him in case Jack saw him there. She heard the tractor starting up and Jack driving it to the entrance to the field. She could never stay in the house when he was ploughing. She put on her overcoat and went out. She followed the tractor all the way up the lane and watched Jack bouncing up and down on the seat. It was a cold morning, but not as cold as it had been recently. Jack would always plough this time of year in order to sow into the dust later on. The morning sunlight was thin and white and dancing dangerously along the plough's blades. Martha thought of Judy.

The ploughshare was cutting through the earth like butter, bringing up red earth to the surface. She stood watching Jack let the plough down by the gate and then he started to work. Her stomach turned too, with every clod of earth. There weren't many big stones in this field since they'd been lifted and thrown into the hedgerows ages ago. Martha could never believe how quickly the lot got turned. She looked up to see the seagulls starting to arrive. She marvelled at how they could know who was ploughing when they lived so far out to sea. Probably there was quite a bit of ploughing going on so they were in the area already. There were about three to begin with, then six and then the air was thick with them, rolling like surf over the brown waves. They'd land and winkle out the worms with their beaks. They looked too clean to go anywhere near the soil. Sometimes there'd be a big hoo-ha when two or three of the birds fancied the same snack. One would try and steal it from the other's beak, then the first would attack and take it back, their shrieks echoing around the neighbourhood. She smiled because it seemed such a big quarrel over such a small prize. She looked at Jack whose head had swivelled backwards to keep an eye on the plough.

Martha felt suddenly seasick. She went to lean on the gate. She looked up in the direction of the hedge under the big oak; the hedge showed no signs of new life. The tractor came closer to the hedge with every row of sod it turned, and each inch made her dizzier. Even though each time she'd know the plough would never touch the hedge, still her chest would always tighten. While she had a thousand and one other things she should be getting on with, she could never even think of leaving the field. Jack had peeled back the field's skin in one long strip by now, the red showing fiercely through. It had to be done. Flaying the skin and leaving it all to bleed like raw meat so as to bring it back to life. Then he would level the field and run the harrow over it to get the earth ready. The whole process was really like baking a cake. Mixing the ingredients, rolling the dough, preparing it, then fertilising it in a floury cloud of lime.

The sound of the seagulls filled the air, attracting more of them to feed on the flesh each furrow uncovered. Martha held her head in her hands. There was something quite unnatural about seeing seagulls so far from their habitat. After about an hour, she noticed Jack had slowed down and turned off the engine. He was walking up and down the rows of sods, splitting the odd clod of earth that had refused to separate. The sound of the spade's iron slicing the roots went right through her. She turned towards the house to boil the kettle for Jack's flask of tea.

Jack stood watching Martha walk away as though she wasn't touching the ground. From this distance she looked like she did when she was fifteen. The straight back and dark hair. Time had made her hair a little white and her cheeks a little ruddy, but the way she withstood age was almost unnatural. It wouldn't be long before dinner. Another half an hour after dinner and he would have finished. Jack enjoyed the smell of the earth and shoed away the odd seagull.

He'd be going to stay with Judy tonight in the council house. Those sullen boys of hers had gone to be with their father. The house was so different to his home at Graig-ddu: light and modern. He could almost pretend to be somebody else while he was there. He raised his head to watch Martha's figure shrinking as she approached the house, then he looked at the big oak in the top hedge. He looked back again and saw her in the distance like a little bird; he breathed in deeply.

FOURTEEN

Tap, tap, tap. Ta-, ta-, ta-, tap.

Martha woke up. She looked at the clock. Half past four in the morning.

Tap, tap, tap, tap.

Someone was trying to get into the house. The sound of somebody running on the landing. The bedroom door opened. Shanco was standing there in his underwear.

'S... s... someone's m... making a noise at the window.' He was shifting from one foot to the other.

She sat up.

Tap. Tap. Tap. Bang. Bang. Bang!

She motioned for him to jump into her bed. His skin was white as wax. She got up and pulled on a cardigan over her nightie. Jack was supposed to be with that woman tonight and maybe he'd wanted to come home early. But he didn't need to knock. The back door was never locked.

Tap, tap, bang! Bang!

If it was Jack, he'd be shouting. No one was shouting either. It could be Gwynfor, Martha thought. But no, not at half past four. She went to the door and opened it carefully. He was shaking on the bed with the blankets pulled tight under his chin.

'M... m... maybe it's the Wh... White Lady,' he said, his eyes like saucers.

The sound seemed to be coming from downstairs. The landing was quiet. She paused and listened, then she went on tiptoe to Jack and Shanco's room and bent under the bed to reach the gun that was kept there. She checked it was loaded and took it back to the top of the stairs.

Tap, tap, tatatata tap!

Sometimes there would be an especially startling bang. The noise now seemed to be shifting from room to room. She started walking downstairs, one hand on the gun and the other on the banister, which looked in the shadow cast on her nightie like a big beast's backbone with spindles for ribs. The moon bled a strange light into the scene. She reached the bottom of the stairs and went to the back door to open it slowly, keeping one hand tight on the gun. There was no one there and the yard was silent. She shut the door slowly and turned towards the pantry. Her bare feet were cold on the slates. Something by the door rustled. Martha turned around. A mouse feeding in one of the cake sacks. She opened the parlour door. Nothing, only the fox's face laughing down at her from the wall through the darkness.

She considered going back to bed.

Tap, tap, tap! Bang! Tap!

The sound was coming from upstairs. She ran to the bottom of the stairs and saw Shanco coming down them crying.

'Th… th… the noise is upstairs now!'

The sound was moving from window to window both upstairs and down.

'Don't be silly, Shanco, there's a good boy; must be someone playing a joke, you'll see.'

She thought about what Jack had said. 'Don't expect an easy ride here from now on.'

'Go to bed now, Shanco.'

'B… b… but maybe it's the Wh… White Lady!'

'Don't pull my leg now.'

His eyes widened even further.

'M... maybe it's M... Mami.'

'Be quiet. I hope you don't really believe in that nonsense. Now go to bed. I'll wait here and make sure no one comes in.'

He was even paler than usual and was kneading the material of his long johns. After a while he nodded and went towards the stairs. He looked back at Martha, his mouth open to speak.

'Go to my bed for tonight.'

He looked a little happier as he slowly climbed the stairs.

Shanco gone, she turned towards the stove. She poured water into a cup and made tea with a teabag. Through the window the garden was still. There was no wind, not a smick of sound. She sat at the table with the gun still in her lap. She decided there was no point going back to bed because he would be fast asleep and the morning was closer than the night by now. The steam from the cup curled slowly into the night; the sounds of morning had started to stir. Her feet were cold on the lino and she fetched a pair of clean socks that had been airing above the stove. She put the gun down on the table and put on the socks awkwardly then went to the door and pulled on her wellingtons too before sitting back down on the settle. She took hold of the gun again and nursed it between her arms and her legs. The kitchen was quiet except for the odd sly movement from the cake sack. She'd have to remember to put poison down there. She thought again of Jack and Judy.

After about half an hour she got up and went to the back door. The darkness was starting to turn a kind of light grey. She opened the door and went out. It was quite mild considering it was early spring. She stepped out into the garden, her wellingtons dampened by the dew. She paused a moment and then put the gun down beside her so that she could look at the ground under the bowl. She crouched, lifted the bowl like an old scab and looked at Gwynfor's footprints. The pattern was as clear in the earth as someone's spirit after the body had gone. She ran her finger along both silhouettes. A little of the ice melted within her and a tear fell from her dark eyes.

FIFTEEN

'I want my breakfast now! Got to get them pens done an' the ram in the shed's got 'is horns turning into 'is 'ead.' Jack had finished milking early, probably because he'd got home earlier than usual. 'Come on then.' Martha had gone back to bed to doze for half an hour and she'd gone back to sleep. 'Wha's wrong with you today?'

She broke the egg into the frying pan and watched the clear liquid turn white.

'I don't know why, but I'm tired, Jack.'

'Go to bed earlier then, for God's sake. You're like a zombie.'

'I went to bed early but something woke me up.'

She slid the fishslice under the egg and turned it over. The yolk broke.

'What the 'ell you talking about, eh?'

She looked at him under heavy lids. 'You tell me, Jack,' she said quietly.

'Wrong in the 'ead, you are. You're going soft, that's what. That egg ready?'

Shanco came in from feeding the calves and went to sit by the fire. There came a clip-clip on the lino and Bob, all muddy, jumped into his lap. Martha put the plate in front of Jack. It was a cold morning; the steam from the food mingled with his breath. Shanco was starting to nod off.

Jack grabbed the ketchup and hit Shanco with it. Bob jumped out of the way just in time.

'Oi! That's enough, you lazy slob. Time you earned your keep round 'ere. Think it's an 'oliday camp?' Shanco looked at him quietly, the swelling visible under his eye. 'Need the slate and a blow torch this mornin' so's we can do that ram.' Shanco nodded. 'Need to heat up the 'orns first so's we can turn them out or they'll screw right into 'is 'ead.' Jack was talking and clearing his plate mechanically at the same time. 'Saw a ram once with its 'orns gone straight into 'is 'ead. Lost on the mountain and no one seen 'im. Went off 'is 'ead.'

Martha looked at the yolk on her plate and put her knife and fork down.

'That's what happens, see, if you leave things like that to fester,' he said.

Jack finished his breakfast and let his knife and fork fall, not bothering to leave them tidily on the middle of his plate. He dried his mouth with a hanky from his pocket, black as his waistcoat. He went back into his pocket to look for his tobacco. He took some paper from his other pocket. He put it on the table and poked it towards Martha.

''Ere, look.'

She looked at the paper in surprise. 'What is it?'

'Want you to take it to town when you go... to the Social.'

She took the paper and opened it, took a little time to look it over. She glanced at Jack. 'And what's this for?'

'Well I've got a bad back, 'aven' I? Can't work properly anymore so we might as well get something back from the sods.'

'You're going to tell them you can't work?'

'Shouldn't 'ave to work so hard anyway. If I 'ad more 'elp about the place my back wouldn't be this bad.'

'I can't take this to town or anywhere else.' She folded the paper and pushed it back across the table.

'Really? Well maybe we'll have to tell Judy to go to town every week instead of you, since it's my car you use, and then you can stay 'ere at 'ome every day.' Martha thought of the café for a moment, of walking through the market. Jack looked at her. 'Judy said it wouldn't take you long to change your mind.'

'I thought *she*'d have something to do with this business. This family's never begged a penny off anyone before.'

'Well more fool us then, that's what I say. Every other fucker's at it. Bloke in the village got a bran' new car. Buggers off on 'oliday three times a year and who's paying? Morons like us. Nothing wrong with 'im. Everyone knows that but no one says a bloody thing.'

'But it's not right, Jack.'

'Farmer over the other side o' Bryn Bach, claims a fortune. Goes out middle of the night to do the farming! Owly, everyone calls 'im, but 'e lives like a fuckin' king!'

'But what if you get caught, Jack?'

'You think they care, Martha? Just take them forms in and that's an end to it. I need extra help outside 'ere this mornin' too. Get goin'. His nibs won't do the job right, will he.'

Jack and Shanco went out to the shed while Martha cleared up. She dried her hands quietly and put on her wellingtons. Turning at the door she looked at the table where the white paper still lay, a clear cloud of grease spreading over a corner.

The ram was in a shed on its own. A big mountain ram with horns standing proud, quite still in the middle of the hay with its eyes fixed on some intolerable pain deep inside. Each side of its head there was a red wound where the horns, which had once made it such a beautiful creature, were curling their way into its skull. She couldn't imagine a worse death.

She went to the ram and took hold of its back while Shanco was clamping down on its back legs. Jack grabbed the ram and put the slate under the horn and as far as he could across its eyes. He started to heat the horn slowly, and in a while they could smell something like glue. Slowly he pulled the horn outwards, the ram meanwhile struggling even harder in pain. She was almost jealous of the ram for having shrugged off its burden so easily. She noticed Judy watching them from the door of the shed. She was wearing overalls, and her strawlike locks were pulled away tight to the top of her skull.

She had started coming to Graig-ddu lately during the day, though it wasn't so she could do much work. She would ride with Jack in the tractor or help Shanco feed the calves and the sheep in the stalls. One evening when Martha went into the milking parlour, there was Jack teaching her how to put the milking machine onto the cow's udder. She let the ram go and walked past Judy towards the house. Judy smiled without looking at her and went towards Jack.

Martha started getting dinner ready and went to the dresser to fetch eggs. There was a knock at the door. She was startled. She went to the door, her chest tight, expecting to see Judy.

'Mrs Martha Williams?' It was a man in blue overalls with a clipboard. There was a big white lorry in the yard, backed up as close as possible to the door.

'*Miss* Williams. Yes,' she answered in Welsh, then corrected it to English.

The man smiled and said in Welsh, 'Delivery for you, *Miss* Williams.' He ran his finger down one of the forms in his hand.

'But... I haven't ordered anything,' she hesitated.

There were two other men busy opening the back of the lorry. The first one looked a bit confused.

'Um... Miss Martha Williams, Graig-ddu Farm....'

She nodded.

'That's what it says on here anyway, love. Sign here then please.'

She didn't like the way he called her 'love', seeing as she was old enough to be his mother. She took the biro offered her and signed shakily on the line. Shanco appeared, all ears. The back of the lorry opened fully and the men started unloading slowly.

'Right then *Missy*,' the man said with a smile, 'Where d'you want this piano?'

The piano was carried into the parlour and set against the wall backing the pantry. The three of them found it hard carrying it safely in under the low doors but soon it was in its place.

'Maybe you should get someone to tune it now, love,' the man said with a wink. 'You know how these old things get a bit cranky if you handle them too much.'

They didn't want a cup of tea because they were calling at some industrial estate next, and the three left as abruptly as they had arrived. Martha made herself some, and sat on the pink sofa to drink it so that she could look at the piano properly. It was a fine one too. Black, and shiny all over like a new penny. She got up and closed the keyboard lid and stood there admiring it. The piano smiled back at her. A wide, friendly smile. She didn't dare touch any of the keys. She saw that Shanco was watching her through the window, and she waved at him to go back to his work. The morning disappeared in a fug of washing clothes and tidying, but she would often pop her head around the parlour door to admire the piano, and every time she did this the piano would smile back at her.

'And what's that great 'ulk of a thing doing in the parlour then?' Jack asked at teatime, smiling at Judy. 'Who the hell's goin' to play that? Them ghosts Shanco's been tellin' me about?'

'It was a present from Gwynfor, Jack.'

'Well, well, Gwynfor's offloadin' all 'is old stuff in one go, is 'e? What'd 'e do with a piano? Typical Gwynfor, that, throwing money away on somethin' that's no use to nobody.'

'It's me that's going to learn it.'

Jack burst out laughing and turned to English, 'She's going to learn to play the piano!'

Judy began to laugh with him.

'B... b... bet M... Martha *can* play,' Shanco said from his chair by the fire.

Jack laughed louder, explaining to Judy, 'And that fuckin' idiot thinks she'll be good at it!'

Judy's laughter sounded as though it were raining shards of glass. 'Well it'd be somethin' for 'er to get on with now she's on her tod, like.'

Martha looked at Shanco. He looked as if he were struggling to stop himself speaking.

'Look, Jack, duck, I reckon' 'e's tryin' *not* to say anythin'! Makes a change – usually he can't get his gob round a sentence, even!'

Shanco got up and Martha got up automatically too.

'Y...y...y,' unusually, Shanco seemed to be trying English words, 'You.' Jack and Judy were laughing even harder. 'Y... y... yo.. you're a bitch!' Shanco shouted, shaking all over.

The smile disappeared from the couple's faces. Martha looked at Shanco, astonished. Jack got up and went over to him, grabbing him by his collar before he had time to escape.

'What,' he spat out in Welsh, 'did you say?'

Jack shook Shanco back and fore as though he were shaking a dog.

Shanco reverted to Welsh, 'Sh... she *is* a bitch!'

Jack hit him in the face until he fell headlong to the ground. As he lay there, he aimed a kick at his belly. Bob was barking wildly and baring his teeth at Jack. Martha watched the whole thing, frozen to the spot. She noticed a little blood dribbling from Shanco's ear and dripping quietly onto the lino.

Jack turned around and pulled Judy up by her hand from her place on the settle. 'And don't you dare take that dimwit to the doctor either, or you'll be fuckin' sorry.'

Martha knelt down by Shanco and put his head in her lap. His face was pale and he looked at her as though she were miles away.

After he'd slammed the door she heard Jack kicking the bowl in the garden and the couple walked right through Gwynfor's footprints to the car.

SIXTEEN

Tap, tap, ta-ta-ta-ta tap.

It was four in the morning. Martha hadn't even slept because she was waiting for the noise to start.

Tap, tap, tap, ta-ta-bang-tap.

She held her head in her hands. She felt as weak as a ghost. The familiar sound of Shanco's feet came from the landing and then he jumped into the far side of the bed, half his face one black bruise. He didn't even look at her. Her back hurt more than usual and the heavy cold she had split her whole body each time she coughed. Shanco had stuck toilet paper into his ears and put his head under the pillow to shut out the noise she was making.

Martha got up slowly. Her cold had made her shaky on her feet, and her legs were aching all over. But she'd put out her clothes ready before going to bed, since tonight she had a plan. She got dressed and put her shoes on: she had worked out that Jack and Judy would have had to knock on the windows with something long like a brush handle or piping, since she hadn't seen any footprints around the house. Even the upper windows weren't that high, what with Cae Berllan field levelling half way up the outside wall, so reaching the window would pose no problem. She took the torch and went quietly downstairs, each time feeling with her feet for the next step. She went into the parlour. She had decided to sit and watch in the parlour to get evidence. She reckoned she'd catch them if she sat long enough at one window. They'd make a mistake, show their faces, sooner or later. Stealth and patience were all that were needed. She thought enviously of Shanco sleeping soundly in the bedroom.

Tap, tap, tap ta-ta-ta-ta tap.

A noise in the bedroom.

The big piano was smiling at her, the moon lighting up its white teeth. She pulled the piano stool out of the way, to the side of the window. That way no one would see her from outside. She sat and watched.

Bang, bang, bang.

Downstairs by the back door. Every knock felt like the echo of a heartbeat in her chest. The fox was laughing at her heartily from above the door. She needed sleep, her breathing rasped, and sometimes her head would fall wearily to her chest. The floral curtains would move now and then in the draught that cut through the glass and the windowframe.

Tap, tap, tap.

It was by the parlour window. Martha woke with a jolt and got up. She could see someone's shadow by the window.

Bang, bang, bang, ta-ta-ta-ta tap.

She caught hold of the curtain and moved her face very slowly forward to see who was there.

Bang, bang, bang, bang.

Black eyes and wings the colour of petrol.

Bang, bang, bang, bang, bang.

An enormous crow clamouring to come in. Her heart skipped.

Bang, bang, bang, bang, bang.

It was hitting the window so hard its beak was all bloody, and the blood was splattering over the window. Its beak had made scratches in the blood on the glass. The red at the base of the beak was spurting into its eyes. It saw her from the corner of its eye and it flew away like a witch into the night. Through the dirty window she watched it leave, and she felt the fox and the piano smirking behind her.

Once her heart had slowed down, she closed the curtains. She ran into the kitchen, letting the torch fall from her lap. She went to the pantry windows and the back door and drew all the curtains. She hadn't done this since Mami's body came back to the house: you didn't generally need to draw the curtains deep in the countryside. Martha had had a shock and felt she'd got even weaker. Her coughs sounded like someone sawing logs. She put on her coat over her clothes and went upstairs to the bedrooms. She closed the curtains in Jack and Shanco's room and went into her own room and saw Shanco sound asleep in her bed; she drew the curtains there too. He was sleeping like a corpse on his back, his mouth wide open and curls of toilet paper poking out of his ears.

On the landing she dithered a moment then turned back towards Mami's room. Martha stood outside the door then raised the latch slowly and went in. This was the most spacious room in the house. It had a massive fireplace on one side and heavy furniture against each wall, dark pieces standing guard in the house's stronghold. She had left it all as it had been the day Mami left them. She went across the room and closed the thin drapes, but still a little light filtered in like sun through water. She went over to the bed and for the first time since losing Mami, she sat down on it. She looked around her. She avoided going into this room unless she needed something. Her talc and comb were still on the little table, the nightie folded over the arm of the chair, the chamberpot still at the foot of the bed. A pair of Dat's galoshes were on the far chair.

Since Christmas Martha had moved all Mami's jewellery into her room just in case things started going missing again. They didn't have many clothes but what they had was still hanging in the two wardrobes flanking the bed. Mami had divided her clothes: those she used to wear when Dat was alive and those worn after he'd gone. Her clothes had fitted her well and she was proud of how trim she'd kept all her life. She wouldn't buy many, but when she did they were expensive ones that could last for years.

Mami hadn't got any posh frocks anyway. She'd even got married in a navy utility suit. Everybody gave her clothes stamps as a wedding present so she could buy the material to make the suit. It didn't have a lining either but Mami hoped no one would notice. Once she'd married Dat and as things started to get easier, she stopped buying any outfit that wasn't lined properly. There wasn't many of Dat's clothes in the wardrobe since Jack had used most of them on the farm to save them buying new everyday clothes. Of course that was after losing Mami. Jack had worn Dat's clothes once after he had gone, and gave Mami such a shock when she saw him coming into the house that she was ill in bed for over a week. It didn't matter once Mami had gone, although Martha'd had a bit of a turn when she saw Jack doing the fencing in Dat's old funeral suit. Mami's clothes didn't fit Martha because Martha was a hulking great lump, according to her mother. Someone must have been walking over Martha's grave: she started to shiver so much that she was unconsciously rubbing her arms to warm them.

From her room she heard Shanco sighing in his sleep. She settled back more comfortably on the bed, leaning back on the headboard. She closed her eyes; the bed was deep and welcoming. She thought of the crow, its hard dark eyes shining like flint ready to spark, and fear shot its load of tiny needles into her body. Mami always said that if a bird tried to get in, someone in the house would die. Dat would scoff at it as old wives' tales, but Mami was sure there was something in the saying. She said some old gent near Llannon had complained a seagull was trying to get into his house and was knocking away all the time, driving him wild. He didn't take long, poor thing, in fact he'd died within the week and no one had sight or sound of that seagull from that time on. Mami said a bird in the house was a surer sign even than corpse candles. To have a wild creature trying to get into your house like that was even more unnatural than an apparition. That crow had been annoying them for weeks: it was a bad omen.

She thought about the crow. It wasn't that it was trying to see its own reflection in the window: it had attacked on cloudy nights as well as clear ones. It wasn't even nesting season either, and she was sure no one was feeding it. There was no explanation for it unless the crow was out of its mind, knocking and knocking away until it drew blood. She hid her face in her hands. The whole thing was disgusting, abnormal. Watch out, they'll be round to measure someone up before too long, you'll see. That's what Mami said about the man from Llannon....

Martha pulled the blankets snug about her and tried to stifle her thoughts in the coverlet. She aired Mami's bed regularly, and when Jack asked her why, she always answered, in case we get visitors sometime who need a place to stay. Jack wouldn't go near the room in any case.

She'd have to wash all the windows tomorrow and decide

69

what to do with the crow. It'd mean a proper scrubbing, because she'd hate it if someone called round and saw the windows all dirty like that.

Her eyes were heavy. Maybe she could get Shanco to help so the job would be over before Jack came back to do the milking, just in case he cursed even worse than usual. She shut her eyes and tried to slow the thoughts darting like little birds through her mind. After about an hour some sort of restless sleep came, full of dreams of Mami and Dat and a big black crow.

Outside it was getting light and the cattle were starting to head towards the milking parlour. On the council estate Jack was starting to wake and think about getting on home. He looked at his clothes, a scrambled bundle by the bed. The work trousers and check shirt and dirty waistcoat looked out of place on the clean light blue carpet. At Graig-ddu Shanco was still straight as a corpse while Bob jumped and jerked in his sleep. Martha slept on in her uneasy sleep, her lungs whispering with each breath. As the darkness dispersed, the birdsong intensified. In the garden a large dark crow was on a branch, its eyes fading in the weak light.

SEVENTEEN

Killing the crow was going to be difficult, Martha thought as she chopped vegetables for soup. She'd fetched the turkey neck from the freezer the night before and already made the stock. She couldn't kill the crow through the window, and it would be hard to catch it outside because they were so canny at sensing danger. Scrubbing the small saucepan clean in the sink with the Brillopad, she thought of John Penbanc's old trick. He would cut up a sponge into small pieces, he said, and smother them in marmite. That way the crows would scoff them up and choke. But on the other hand, she thought, chances were that other birds would swallow them too. Or she could borrow an alarm that would sound off every half an hour or so, but since the crow was near the house, that would keep everyone awake. Maybe she should leave one window open some night so it might come in. Maybe she should clean up Mami's room and move everything out; trap it in there. That would be the way to catch it good and proper.. But thinking of the crow coming into the house sent a shiver up her spine. Poison? Perhaps that might be the answer.

You could hear a car in the yard. There was someone there. Martha dried her hands and put on the stove the pan of soup with its leeks bobbing in the stock and turning like loose eyeballs. She put the lid on. She expected a knock at the door.

Beep, beep!

A car horn. She looked at the clock. It was a little early for the baker who called every week. She went to the door and walked out into the yard where there was a 4x4 – a new one, shiny and enormous. She looked again to see who was in it. A voice came from the passenger seat.

'What you reckon, eh Martha?'

It was Judy, her eyes smiling. Jack turned off the engine, opened the door and stepped out.

'Don't start, I'm warnin' you,' he said to Martha.

Martha looked at him. Shanco appeared, the two strips of toilet paper still hanging from his ears. Bob was jumping around him and barking, looking up at the paper fluttering in the wind.

'But,' Martha began.

'Never 'ad anything like this before, and we're not getting' any younger. Bugger it, I say,' Jack told her.

Shanco was walking around the vehicle, smiling. He tentatively touched the silver paint with one finger. He drew back his hand as though the metal were scorching, then he touched it again. Stress was pulling down the lines of Martha's face.

'But we can't afford...'

'Well it's done now and that's an end to it. We've all got to 'ave somethin' to live for: I deserve a treat after all the hard work I've done.'

'What about all the things that need doing around here? The milking parlour's falling to bits and we're desperate for a new tractor!'

Jack stood toe to toe with her. 'What is the point, Martha, of improving stuff like that? What is the point? None of us'll be here long anyway; might as well live it up a bit, I say.'

Judy was climbing out the other side.

'But you've still got the new car?' Martha said as Jack walked past her towards the house. He looked back at her.

'This is much more like Jack's kind of thing,' Judy said, 'I reckon, anyway. Me son can't get enough of Jack's old banger. Seventeen next week, he is. Luvly pressie for 'im, don' you reckon?'

Martha stuck to Welsh. 'But Jack, how will I get to town to get my jobs done? I could never drive that big lump of a thing, and my back....'

Jack looked at Judy.

'Judy'll 'ave to take you, that's all.'

'What?'

'Judy can give you a lift every week. Don't make a big fuss about it now, for God's sake.'

'But why'd we need something like this, Jack? It's not as if we ever go anywhere, is it?'

'Maybe not, but Judy gets about.'

He turned his back and Judy went after him towards the house. Shanco was looking through the window into the boot. The paint looked so clean against the cowshed wall. Shanco looked at Martha and smiled.

EIGHTEEN

Neither said a word to one another all the way into town. Judy didn't want to be giving Martha a lift, but then again it was too good a chance to get one up on her and get Martha to depend on her. Martha didn't want to be driven either, but she had to go to town. Judy waited outside every shop, impatiently leaving the engine running.

Martha took her time in each place, waiting for the first time in ages to chat to Mr Huws. Every week he'd get Shanco's pills ready, his hang-dog eyes looking at Martha over his half-moon glasses. She waited to talk to the butcher as he weighed the meat and plopped it into clear plastic bags, waving his wrist to twist them shut. She could hear the throaty engine growling at her outside each shop.

'Get me some tabs from the Newsie, will you?' Martha looked at her. She'd never bought cigarettes in her life. 'Lambert and Butlers, twenty.'

She didn't know what she had to do, nor what to ask for. Judy looked at her, exasperated.

'D'you want a lift to town with me or what?' Martha paused. 'Jack'll give you the dosh after.'

Her cheeks went scarlet as she ordered the cigarettes. Usually all she'd ask Emyr Shop for was the local paper and a packet of mints for Shanco. Daily Post was Emyr's other nickname; the news was more than just his livelihood.

'Well, well, pretty good times for farmers, isn't it?

'What do you mean, Mr Williams?'

'Driving round in these 4x4s. EU must be looking after some of us anyway. All they're interested in doing for me is taking the bend out of bananas.' He leaned over to have a look at the car, past the posters in the window. He sucked his teeth. 'Must be twenty thousand's worth there, isn't there? Must be in the wrong bloody job.'

Martha picked up the cigarettes and pushed them to the bottom of her bag.

'That's the woman, is it?' Emyr winked at Martha. 'Bit of hot stuff, so I hear... fond of camping, so they say!' She hadn't the heart to ask him to elaborate, or to ask who the gossips were. That would have been too much to take.

'Jack's worked hard all his life. I'd say he's a right to get a new car if he needs one.' Her ears were burning.

'I'm not saying anything, Martha,' Emyr noticed her expression and coughed before going on, 'er, Miss Williams... just keep an eye on her, that's all,' he said, raising his eyebrows suggestively.

'And what exactly is that supposed to mean, Mr Williams?'

Emyr bent forward and whispered, even though there was no one in the shop. 'Watch her, that's all... in case, you know,' She looked at him, 'in case it's not the king she fancies, but the castle.'

Martha took the mints and the paper and put them in her bag. 'Good morning, Mr Williams,' she said as the bell clanged behind her.

On the way home the car went down Bridge Street, past Eurwen's café. Martha noticed through the steamy window that it was busy in there today. She saw the café pass like a dream. That was the first time in years that she hadn't been in there Thursday afternoon. Apart from those two snowy winters in the Sixties and the Eighties, she'd attended the place every week like chapel. Would anyone notice that she hadn't gone there today? They must have, surely.

Judy was smoking a fag and turning the music in the car right up. Martha noticed her nails: yellow, long and hard, like a cat's. She had on an old tracksuit, riding boots and fingerless gloves. She'd made no effort to smarten up for their visit to town. Martha started to cough at the smoke, but Judy only looked at her and smiled.

'Did you get Jack's money, duck?' she asked, sucking the last gasps from the cigarette until the tip glowed red. Fetching Jack's money had become a weekly source of shame. It was the talk of the town, the tattle squealing like swifts swinging through the square. Martha sensed a second's heavy pause in the shops as she entered. At least Emyr had the guts to tell her to her face what everyone else was thinking. Nobody had ever had a word against her family before, as far as Martha knew.

The smoke was starting to make her feel sick. She wasn't used to being a passenger, and the music was throbbing inside her head, so hard she felt faint. Judy looked at her.

'I'm going... I'm going to be sick.'

Judy braked hard and the car came to a sudden stop. The front wheel got stuck in the verge and they turned with a screech to face the hedge.

'Fuck,' Judy shouted, leaning over Martha to open the far door. 'Get out, don't fuckin' puke in 'ere.' She clutched the sides of the seat and tried to keep it down. 'Get out, for God's sake. We're right in the middle of the road. Something might hit us.'

It was a long step down; Martha's legs were weak and stiff. She managed to get both feet on the ground and emptied out her stomach onto the grass. Judy moved the car forward a little along the road. Martha's face was all red; she looked for a hanky but she hadn't got one. The pockets of her best suit were still sewn right up to keep the line of the jacket. She tried to spit the sick from her lips, looking around all the while in case anyone came by. She walked to the car and Judy started up the engine, looked at Martha and lit another cigarette.

'God it stinks in 'ere now.'

Martha quickly took off her navy suit. Her work clothes were by the bed. She took off her petticoat and tights and put on a heavy jumper and trousers. She felt better by now and put the suit in the laundry basket. She looked in the mirror and saw that a little colour had returned to her cheeks.

She went back to the kitchen, put on her wellingtons and went out to the yard. Bob was there, playing with Shanco, who ran over to her. She stopped. Shanco was all smiles.

'Wh... wh... what you doin'?' Bob was trying to jump up and bite his fingers.

'Now then Shanco, you've got to go over to the big shed and have a look at those sheep in there. Make sure every lamb is suckling, got to tie up the big one in Number Three, stop her kicking the little lamb. You listening?'

His shoulders broadened with the weight of responsibility. Martha knew from the way he was nodding his head that he was silently repeating her words as he went to do the job. He ran over to the big shed. Jack had nearly finished skinning a lamb by the dog shed, sliding the knife between the skin and the small pink skeleton. When he'd done, he threw the flesh for dogfood into some old bucket before fetching the orphan lamb from a box at his feet. He fitted the skin over the limbs of the live lamb like it was a little jacket. She ignored him as she walked past.

She went to the storehouse, climbed the slate steps, took the key from her pocket and unlocked the door. She pushed open the door: the mice shot deep into the darkness. The dust was white sparks in the light rays, radiating. Martha stepped in. The storeroom was a graveyard of old stuff. Old furniture; fancy chairs they hadn't found room for in the house; snares; rusted mousetraps; the old saddle of carthorses long since put out to grass; horseshoes as big as dinner plates; old biscuit tins full of screws and nails, decorated with lovely pictures of flowers and pretty women. Slowly her eyes got used to the dark. Along one wall were wooden shelves sagging under the clutter. She waded over to them, and on the bottom shelf was an old flower oasis, its plastic letters spelling a name. The flowers had wilted a while back; the oasis still as green as the plastic. A curl of plastic pink ribbon was tied behind the letters. Martha's chest tightened. She shifted her fingers along the shelves, trailing a drift of dirt; eyes rivetted on the rubbish. Then she found it. A little white plastic bottle whose yellow cap was grey under the dust. Martha rubbed her finger across the label so she could read it. Strychnine alkaloid (0.5%). She smiled. This should do the job. She wiped the bottle and went to sit in one of the fancy chairs. Her back ached. She sat there a while holding the bottle tight and looking at the green plastic letters still spelling 'Mami' in the darkness.

Strychnine is pretty odd stuff, you know. Not dangerous until mixed with water. A lot of poison was like that – a bit like people, in a way – totally innocent until mixed with certain other people. That was when things got out of hand. She looked at the bottle with its cap like a crown of yellow hair. She mixed the powder into water as though she were stirring gravy, holding her breath all the while. She put down the poison. She closed the bottle. She put it into her pocket and wiped the table with a cloth, throwing it into the bin afterwards.

Martha heard Jack and Judy coming into the house. She had got tea ready for them, leaving the plates on top of the stove. She wasn't at all hungry. She went upstairs and into her room before they opened the door.

She undressed and put on her nightie, then went to the window to close the curtains. It was terribly windy outside, the branches scraping at the sky. She heard the chatter and cackles of laughter from the kitchen. They must enjoy nights like this when Martha wasn't there and Shanco was feeding the animals late. Once Martha had taken a little cough medicine, she put out the light and got into bed. Her cough was no better and her inability to rest just made everything worse. The medicine was sweet as treacle on her teeth.

She dozed quietly; from afar she heard the sound of Shanco going to bed early and the tick-tick of Bob's claws on the landing. He had remembered to take him into his bedroom, just like Martha had told him. Sleep was dragging her far down into the flab of the ticking mattress. She had a fever, but at the same time she was certain for the first time that at least from now on she could have some rest. Her sleep was as sweet as the medicine, the deepest she had ever had, approached so certainly that her limbs weighed heavy and every bone in her body relaxed. She slept like a corpse, hardly breathing. She would take some waking. Her sleep was so deep she neither heard nor felt Shanco coming into her bed in the middle of the night, nor did she hear Bob jumping up and settling in a fat coil at the far end. For once the sound of Jack and Judy leaving passed her by. The tent eyed the house darkly. The bats shot around the yard like poison darts, while the cat assassinated several mice in the haybarn. But Martha was dead to the world.

NINETEEN

It was eight o'clock in the morning, and *Martha* was half awake. She'd slept so much she had a headache. She looked over the other side of the bed and saw the blanket thrown aside with its traces of dog hair at the far end. She tried to sit up. She was stronger today, as though sleep had pumped an hourly supply of fresh blood to her veins. The silence from downstairs seeped up to her. She stood up, realising her balance had improved. She went straight to the window, opened the curtains and looked out. Nothing there. She dressed quickly and went down. Last night's plates were still on the table. Martha put on her shoes and her coat and opened the back door. It was a fine morning, the sun a washed out yellow duster wiping the yard clean. Over on the other side of the yard she heard the milking parlour pumping in, pumping out, like the mechanical heart of the place.

Martha went to the side of the house and into the garden. She looked over at the old bowl lying like a rebuke in the grass. She went behind the house and looked around. Not a trace. She searched inside the rhododendron bush: no sign. She walked up the garden. Nothing except the heads of daffodils who'd showed up like soldiers in an ambush. No crow, nothing. She dithered for a moment, awash with guilt.

She went back to the house to clear the plates from yesterday's tea and start on breakfast. Martha heard the milking machine stop and Shanco banging buckets about as he went to feed the calves. She heard heavy footsteps approaching the house.

'No messin' about today, I'll need help with the dosing.' The milk jug was in Jack's hand. He put it on the table and sat down to look at some papers on the settle. 'You're good at doling out the medicine.'

The words nearly laid Martha out flat. She pretended to look for the saucepan. 'Can't she help you then?'

'If it's Judy you're wittering on about, no she can't, she isn't feelin' too good today.'

'Oh, what a pity,' she answered, lowering the bacon into the frying pan. She fried it without speaking, listening to the fat spattering in the pan. Shanco came into the house with Bob stuffed into his coat. She put out a small plate of egg and bacon for him in his place by the fire. Unusually for her, she paused to stroke Bob, then she turned to give the other plate to Jack.

'You didn't see a crow out in the garden this morning, did you?'

Jack looked up. 'What the hell're you talkin' about?'

'Did you see a crow out in the garden this morning?'

Shanco gripped Bob a little tighter.

'There's thousands of the devils around the place; did you 'ave any particular one in mind?'

'A dead one.'

'You think I 'aven' got anythin' better to do than go running around after some dead crow? One less to worry about, that's all.' Jack went on eating then stopped again to look at her. His eyes narrowed. 'Why?'

Martha pushed the frying pan into the washing up bowl so that the water in it splashed up and clouded the window in steam.

'Oh, nothing really.'

Jack watched her, his eyes like slits.

'Why, what've you done?'

'Nothing, just thought well, there was one there yesterday, and this morning there's no sign of it, that's all.'

He went back to his food. 'Somethin's eaten it, probably.' Martha's stomach lurched. 'Or it's rotted away.'

She wiped the top of the stove, which steamed from the damp of the dishcloth.

'Not that fast, surely?'

Jack threw down his knife and fork. 'Course it'd 'appen that fast. Y'know how many of them birds are flying around 'ere? Ever noticed the dead ones? No one sees them, unless they got knocked down.'

Jack got up and went over to the door. Shanco jumped up too, pressing Bob deep into his jumper. Bob looked all sulky at the way he was being wrapped up tight in the wool.

'Don't be long doin' that now then. Come out in 'alf an hour and we'll 'ave got them in by then.'

The door shut and the kitchen fell silent.

Jack was right too, Martha thought; there were thousands of birds in the air and yet she hardly ever saw any dead ones, apart from the odd one on the road. Where did they all go? Martha slid the dirty crockery quietly into the hot water in the bowl. She wiped the table. Maybe they went somewhere special to die. She turned it over in her head as she dried each plate with care. If she were a bird she'd fly up and up as high as can be before dying.

Maybe it had rotted away, but that wasn't likely in one night. Martha felt her stomach in knots. It seemed as though the crow had never been. She would have liked to have seen the body, seen the feathers and the black eyes. Mami's words hummed in her head like bees. 'That stuff's dangerous, be careful now: it kills seven times over, remember. Seven times over.'

She went over to the door and put on her wellingtons and her coat. Wasn't it odd, she thought, lifting the latch of the back door; odd that the birds were all around Graig-ddu, lived alongside them even, and yet once gone they seldom left a trace.

TWENTY

'Martha!' She gave a start. She was skulking about the garden, still trying to find the crow. 'Martha!' Jack was in a state.

'What?'

'Where are you?'

'The garden.'

She heard his steps getting closer.

'Where?' he yelled out.

She got up from behind a bush. It was Jack's turn to be startled.

'Fuckin' 'ell woman, you got to jump out at me like that? You know what Dr Evans said.'

'What d'you want?'

'Where's the bank books?'

'What bank books?'

'My bank books. Principality, the whole lot.'

'How should I know?'

Jack's face was draining white. 'Well it's you that takes that stuff in for me.'

'So?'

'So where are they?'

Martha just wanted to get back to her search. 'In the dresser drawer, you know, where we always keep them.'

'Looked there.'

'I don't know then, do I?'

She stooped down again and stared into the undergrowth.

'Christ, woman, we've lost the books then, every last fuckin' one of 'em!'

She straightened up. Jack's face was chalky, his hands shaking.

'You've looked for them properly?'

''Course I 'ave.'

Martha came out of the bushes and followed Jack over to the house. She looked in the dresser drawer. No sign. She looked in the table drawers. Nothing. A measure of blood drained from his face for every drawer they found empty.

'The whole fuckin' lot's in them books. Anyone can get the money out; all they'd have to do is take them up to the Midlands or somewhere, forge my signature and I'd be fucked.'

She started fretting. 'Well, I took your money in for you yesterday in town, and then I put them back in here last night.'

'I saw them in the drawer too,' Jack said. ''cause I went to check you'd put them away.'

'When?'

'After tea. You'd gone to bed, Judy was 'aving her tea and Shanco hadn't come in yet.'

'Did you stay in the kitchen the whole time?'

He blushed. 'What you tryin' to say, then?'

'Well we all know who's got the light fingers around here, don't we? *She* was the last one to see you putting them away, and *she* hasn't been here today, has she?'

There was no blood left in his face as he sat down. 'No, never, no way; she wouldn't do it.' Martha sat down too. 'She wouldn't do something like that, don't be so... p'raps she's taken them to look after them... she wouldn't....'

Her heart was beating harder. 'Well you'd better go to

town to put a stop on all those accounts,' she said. Jack's eyes were darting like pistons. 'You'd better do it quick as you can, unless it's too late already.'

Jack's temper flared up. 'Fuckin' 'ell!'

He got up and went over to the door. She went after him and watched him leave. He jumped into the new 4x4, wellingtons and overcoat all covered in shit. She closed the door to the sound of the car screeching up the lane. Martha had been expecting this for ages; really she was surprised how long it had taken for Judy to get what she was after. That was why she'd put her savings in another account months ago. At last Judy had shown her true colours. She smiled.

Martha had to do the milking because Jack was still in town. The cows didn't know her that well and some of the younger ones were jigging about nervously. Time and again she'd had to jump out of the way and one of the heifers had refused to let down her milk. So that she'd have extra time to get a special tea ready, she went to help Shanco feed the calves after the milking was done. The buckets were washed and the pair went back to the house. Shanco sat by the fire and she started peeling the potatoes. They could hear the growl of the 4x4. Martha's chest tightened. The door opened and Jack came in. He threw his coat down on the floor and she saw his wellingtons were wrapped in Tesco bags.

'What a fuckin' palaver. Made me wear these bags over my wellies. Bit o' shit never did no one no harm!'

He took off the bags and the boots and sat down at the table. Martha carried on peeling. She didn't want to be the first to speak. There was the sound of a second car coming in the yard. She peeled faster. Judy came in and sat down. Martha and Jack both looked surprised.

'What the fuck you lookin' at?' Judy exclaimed. 'God, I've felt like crap all day; must 'ave caught your filthy bug.' She looked at Martha. 'Or your cookin' last night, mebbe.'

Martha threw the knife down into the sink. 'How dare you?' Judy looked at her in surprise. 'How dare you come here after what you've done? I don't know how you've got the nerve.'

'Nothing's gone from the bank, Martha,' Jack said privately.

Martha looked at him. 'And what's that supposed to prove? Bet that tramp of a son of hers has got them; must be half way to Birmingham by now.'

'What the 'ell's she on about?' Judy asked Jack. He looked at Martha, at Judy, then down at the table.

'It's… it's just my bank books've gone missing,' he told her.

'And I don't think we need look very far to see who's got them either,' Martha added, a potato still in her hand.

Jack looked at Judy. Both of them went red. She started to tremble.

'And you reckon,' she began, 'you reckon I'm nobbut a thievin' little slapper, do yeh?' Her eyes were sparking as she looked at Jack, 'Wouldn't expect nothin' better from her, but you, Jack?'

Jack was taking a sudden interest in the table. Martha squeezed the potato in her fingers until the blood drained away, leaving the tips like little white tubers.

'J… J…J…'

'Shut your trap, Shanco,' Jack shouted.

'Fine,' Judy got up, 'Bloody great; I come over 'ere feelin' like shit; some fuckin' fine dose of medicine this is.' She went over to the door and slammed it behind her. The family listened to the car starting up then fading into the night.

Shanco got up and came over to the table. He opened his coat and reached deep into his pocket. He pulled out four bank books and put them on the table. He hands were shaking.

'W... w... was j... just keeping them s... safe. D... drawer wasn't sh... shut right. W... was scared s... someone'd take them....'

TWENTY-ONE

Martha pushed her finger into the lamb's mouth. The lamb was freezing cold. She took an old piece of carpet and lined the lower oven with it. She rubbed the lamb with an old towel then laid it down in there to warm up. The lamb was wet; now and then it would stretch out its head. There was no point feeding it until it'd warmed up a little. She went out to the pantry and took a bag of colostrum out of the freezer; she put it in a saucepan on the hotplate. She made herself a cup of tea to drink while waiting for the milk to thaw out. It had been snowing outside; it had melted in pools of dirty water across the lino, where her shoes had carried in the white powder. She noticed a pair of grey wellingtons by the door.

It had started slowly, like the snow. First a stranger's overcoat clinging behind the back door, then grey wellingtons on the doorstep; a jumper strewn on the settle. Gradually her home's landscape was coated with a drift of Judy's things. Martha looked at the jumper left where it had fallen. Usually she'd have tidied it away but she didn't want to touch it since it stank of fag smoke. It wasn't just the house that looked different. There were colourful hair bobbles wound around the 4x4's gear stick, and a new plastic apron in the milking parlour. The flow of her thoughts was stopped by a feeble sound coming from the oven.

Martha finished her tea and poured the colostrum into a baby's bottle, screwed on the teat and sat by the fire. She made sure the milk wasn't too hot by dripping a little onto her wrist. Then she took the lamb and wrapped it in the towel in case it dirtied her apron. She used two fingers of her left hand to open its mouth and pushed in the teat with the other. She squeezed a little milk down its throat to give it a taste. It started to shake his head and suckle weakly. She was glad that at least they'd avoided having to feed it with a tube down its throat.

Its mother had died. Shanco had found it asleep, snuggled up by her side. It wouldn't have lasted long in this weather. Lambs could easily lie there for two or three days before hunger got them moving. Then they'd try and graze or feed on cake and some lambs would live but they'd always be feeble: never come right. Martha dried its head and plucked the tight curls around its neck and ears. It was a strong lamb and would come round with a little care. Bubbles rose in the milk as it suckled and she rubbed the top of its bottom to help it suck. She'd noticed in the past how when a lamb was with its mother the top of its tail was close enough for her to tickle it, encouraging it to suckle. The lamb sucked more greedily. She smiled and touched its head with her lips. It finished the milk and she nursed the lamb a while.

The white flakes had stifled any sound from outside. People seemed to think snow brought silence with it, but for Martha it brought anticipation. That silence always made her feel as though something was about to happen, more than just more snow. She looked out through the window. She saw Jack and Shanco trying to thaw the water pipes in the milking parlour, using buckets out in the yard. Shanco had forgotten to leave them to drip and the whole lot had frozen solid. So of course Jack was in a bad mood. Shanco was quiet too, having been told off by Jack for having spent the morning sledging down Banc Mawr on an old car bonnet. He'd come into the house, soaking wet, at eleven o'clock and his clothes were drying above the stove. Now he was wearing his suit trousers and an old flowery jumper of Martha's. She smiled when she saw him walking with legs a yard apart from each other because he was scared the muck from his wellingtons would spread up his trousers. Jack noticed the way he was walking too and clipped him across the ear. She laughed to see Shanco standing there, trying to follow Jack's instructions, with his legs as far apart as this little lamb's would be once it started to walk. The lamb was asleep.

Martha got up and put it in a cardboard box with a towel under its bottom. She dragged the box over to the fire. Its wool was starting to dry into tight white waves; its belly had stopped trembling. She knew that within the hour it would be on its feet and tripping everyone up around the kitchen.

Hopefully some other ewe would take on the lamb so she wouldn't have to nurse it as a pet lamb, but lambing was nearly over so there were fewer mothers to choose from. She had already looked between its legs to check its sex but unfortunately it was male. This caused problems every year when Shanco nursed them. At least with females Martha could persuade Jack to keep them but males were sent to the slaughterhouse. Every year Jack would make Shanco go into the trailer so that the obedient pet lambs would follow him. In the slaughterhouse they would wait by the gate, sure that they wouldn't face the same fate as the other lambs. Each year Shanco would cry until he made himself ill. Martha suspected the three pet lambs that had got lost last year had had a helping hand across the fence into Will's land at Tyddyn Gwyn. Poor old Shanco didn't realise that once over the fence their hooves would beat a pretty smart march to Will's freezer all the same. She started to unfurl a cabbage for dinner.

'Martha!' Jack's voice came from outside.

She dried her hands on her apron and went over to the back door. She pulled her coat around her shoulders in the hope that it wouldn't take long. She opened the door.

'Martha! Come and see this!'

She took care as she stepped over the step which was slippery as glass. She could hear Jack and Shanco's voices from the bottom of the garden. She walked carefully around the corner and saw them standing around a small body on the ground. She watched them looking down at the fox at their feet.

'What the hell caught this then?' Jack said, kicking it aside. It was a big fox, strong and beautiful, its red fur bright against the snow. Crows had pecked out its eyes already and something had attacked its belly. Her stomach turned.

'I don't know, Jack,' she said, her voice shaking.

Kills seven times over, that's what Mami said.

TWENTY-TWO

Jack opened the shed and let Roy bounce like a ball around the yard. Roy never jumped up at you; that would be bad manners. After his display of joy he came close to his master, staying tight by his legs and looking up eagerly into his face. Jack and Roy walked away, leaving the other dogs snuffling hungrily under the doors. Lambing was coming to an end; after a shaky week of suckling, the new lambs had found their feet and the bottle to prance about among the older ones. Every year they'd play the same games. Running together recklessly as one great wave, along the hedge as far as the corner, and breaking there into a skein of white surf. Or one would jump up onto a sheep that was lying there, to show off to the others. None of the older lambs had shown them these tricks: there were no fat lambs left and even had there been, by now those would have mended their over-energetic ways. Every year the same games, the same instinct. Jack and Roy reached the field and Jack pulled the chain over the post. Making a show of courtesy, Roy waited for Jack to limp though the gate, then he followed him obediently. His eyes were already locked onto the sheep as Jack replaced the chain on the post.

The field was awash with sheep and their lambs, both singletons and twins, all mixed together. Roy's job, once the far gate into the next field was open, was to pick off the mothers with singletons from those with twins and send the latter through the gate. Jack walked towards the far gate with Roy at his heel like iron filings clinging to a magnet. The short pasture was flecked with sheep droppings. There were snags of wool like spit along the barbed wire around the field, where the odd sheep had tried to push itself into neighbouring fields, hoping the grass was greener. Jack opened the gate. The lambs were still playing in gangs and you couldn't tell which sheep belonged to a single or pair of lambs. Jack went to stand in the middle of the field with his back towards the open gate. He leaned on his stick. As the sheep raggedly went for the open gate, Roy lined them up so Jack could see them. Jack whistled and Roy came to heel. Jack didn't look at him but sensed he was there. Jack would whistle by now instead of using instructions like 'away', or 'come by', to save getting a sore throat and so that Roy could hear him from further away. Jack looked at the sheep. Another whistle. Roy got up and moved like the river in flood.

Jack watched him work, letting out a low whistle now and then which would hang in the air between them like an exclamation mark. Roy would go up close enough to the ewes to disturb them, so that they called for their lambs. When he was happy which lamb belonged to which sheep, the dog would split them off from the group. After getting the first ones through, he would follow the same pattern. Trying to keep them calm, he would walk each sheep and her lamb past Jack and through the gate behind him.

Jack loved watching Roy. Leaning on his stick, he let himself drift, enjoying feeling part of a partnership that needed no explaining. An instinctive one, totally natural. He'd only ever had two good dogs like this one. The other, Glen, was a Border Collie too. He'd had pepper and salt ears and a short shiny coat. Jack used to give him an egg each night to keep him sharp. His head was like Roy's too: three long tufts under his chin and the same quick mind.

Jack saw a lame sheep going past, whistled, and Roy split off the little group from the others. Jack looked at the sheep; Roy was standing the other side of her. Jack and Roy exchanged a glance. Jack whistled again and Roy grabbed the wool at the scruff of her neck and pulled her to the ground. She lay there kicking but Roy wouldn't let go. Her lambs were bleating around Roy's legs: they hadn't yet learnt to fear him. Roy let her go once he was sure Jack had hold of her, and Jack turned her over to look at the hoof. The sheep was breathing heavily under Jack's elbow as he pressed into her side. You could see the fear in her eyes, that wild fear Jack couldn't comprehend. He spent his whole time tending his animals but their fear remained. Jack thought of Shanco's eyes when he'd hit him in the kitchen. Jack remembered that look of fear. Roy was standing close, wagging his tail and looking pleased. Jack let the sheep go and went back to the middle of the field.

Glen had been very defensive of Jack. Not in a nasty way; he was just loyal. Whenever Shanco teased him he would always look at Jack to get permission to give him a little nip. He would never give a vicious bite, all he was doing was reminding Shanco of how he could turn nasty should he need to. Glen would also walk between Jack and Gwen. A weight pressed on Jack whenever he thought of her. When they started going out, Glen would bark at her and refuse to settle until she was on her way. After six months or so the dog would let them hold hands but he would walk between them under their clasped hands. He would also sit between them on the settle. None of the dogs except Glen ever got to come into the house. After Dat died, Mami'd say it was like having another man about the place. But Gwen didn't get to come into the house too often after that.

Square peg in a round hole, Mami said. Not good enough. A nurse, I ask you! Nurses had a reputation, anyway, and she'd only run off with some doctor in a tidy white coat, wouldn't she, some boyfriend she wouldn't have to clean up after? And what use would a woman keeping those sort of hours be around a farm? No one around to get meals ready and she'd raise a brood of Mammy's Boys, more than likely. All of a type, them village girls, couldn't muck out a makeup box. She'd look after number one, she would, and spend every penny on fancy stuff she didn't need. Lady Muck swanning around a cowshed! The make-up, all that junk, cost a fair penny. How could Jack keep her in the style she was used to? And you know what they say about them painted ladies, need I say more?

And that's just how it turned out.

Roy was sorting the lambs and sheep quickly, bringing down the number left to about a dozen. Jack noticed one sheep by the hedge with a new-born lamb at her feet. Roy picked out the last ones and Jack closed the gate. Jack decided to let the new lamb stay in the field for the night. He went over to look at it, Roy shadowing him. The sheep was calling to her lamb so softly, as though she were clearing her throat. The lamb, in its coat of yellow slime, floundered a little by its mother. Its head was shaking as though it was in shock, then it began to find its feet. The sheep's eyes fixed on it and she started to lick it, ignoring Jack and Roy standing a stone's throw away. The pink afterbirth hung out of her body like a silk scarf dirtied where it trailed on the ground as she moved. Jack looked at the pair quietly.

Gwen had had a child: a little boy. She'd done well for

herself too. Became a Sister, not done badly at all, from what Jack had picked up from the parish paper. Went to live on Mason's Row. He was a mechanic, so he would have had dirty work for her to clean up after anyway. She'd have had to wash his clothes, all muck and oil.

Jack turned for the gate and walked slowly towards the house.

TWENTY-THREE

'Now then, watch your head and don't let go or I'll fall,' Martha said to Shanco. She teetered backwards down the storehouse steps. The skeleton of the scarecrow was lying like an invalid between their arms. Shanco was concentrating on her every word. The barley had been sown, and ten days later, a bright green shadow was bristling through the soil. A few crows hopped in the branches like notes of music come loose from their stave. 'Put him down, then; careful, now.'

The corpse was let down onto the floor. Shanco had wrapped it up in a blanket for the winter; to keep him warm, he said. Martha looked at the scarecrow. Raising it from its grave each year did nothing to improve its appearance: its guts were spilling out of its dark jacket and in places the straw was falling from its wooden frame like rotten flesh. Shanco was on the verge of tears.

'Don't be silly; all he needs is for us to make him better. Otherwise there'll be no seeds left in that field.'

Martha brought clean straw from the haybarn and Shanco pulled lengths of twine out of the smaller bales. He was quietly getting into the swing of it, his pink tongue poking out of his mouth, his face intent upon his task. Every handful of sustenance added flesh to bones, bringing the scarecrow's humped outline upright onto the cross where it had been ailing. Now and then Bob would appear by Shanco's side to tease him, stealing a knife or a piece of twine until Shanco chased him, laughing. She watched him working and tutted whenever she came across some hole a mouse had made in the jacket. They had given the scarecrow a new suit of clothes years ago, but by now it was a pretty shabby outfit. Shanco had even painted a new face on it with red sheep marker which had run down its face like blood. All it needed for the figure to come to life was a couple of nails driven into the staves. The scarecrow was up on its feet and set leaning against the cowshed wall. She looked at it, smiling; Shanco's smile was wide as a turnip lantern's. After a breather they rolled the figure back up into its blanket and took each end of it, ready for the procession up to Cae Marged. They had to rest every little while for Martha to catch her breath. She had thought of asking Jack to carry it in the tractor's bucket, but he was with Judy and best left to his own devices. At each stop, Shanco would sit in the lane with the scarecrow's head in his lap, chanting out the names of wild flowers growing in the hedge.

'Bird's eye, bluebell.'

It was a mild day; Martha was struggling with the burden.

'Ox-eye daisy, forget-me-not.'

Another rest: 'Black eyes, daisy.'

There was a sheen of sweat on Martha's forehead as she took it up again. Her body started to feel heavy. As they turned into the field, dozens of crows rose like flies off a carcass. The pair walked slowly into the middle of the field, following each other's footsteps to avoid damaging the seedlings. She noticed the crows had settled into the big oak like a threatening dark cloud. That morning Jack had dug a hole for the scarecrow, so all they had to do was push the post in deep enough to resist the wind. They lifted it up and pushed it into the earth, Martha holding it by its feet

100

while Shanco trod hard into the soil around it. She took hold of it and shook it to make sure it was sound.

'Think he'll do alright, Shanco?'

'He's p... pretty,' he answered, smiling broadly. She turned to look behind her. The crows had scattered further off, though a few were huddling on the power line like words strung out in a sentence. She shivered.

'You know what,' Martha looked up at the scarecrow, shielding her eyes, 'I think he could do with a hat.' Shanco's eyes lit up. 'Go and fetch one from the house; Jack's old cap's in the pantry.'

Shanco smiled at her intently as though asking permission. She nodded and he ran fast over to the house, his laughter rising like the dust around him. She watched him go, then she let her gaze drop to the ground. The little heads of barley had come up like bristles through the light brown soil. As the sun sank, Martha found she could comfortably look up at the scarecrow's face. Its head was lolling as though it were lazing in the sun. She wondered whether this was all they'd need to keep the crows away. Last year she had had to shoot the crows and hang them by their legs in trees close to the crop but even that hadn't got rid of them altogether. They would stay away for a few days but then the sky would be black with their screeching and they'd be back. She rubbed her arms to keep warm, the hairs rising like the barley through the field's skin. He was taking a while to come back. The sweat on her back was chilling her now and she decided to return to the house.

Shanco must have got distracted. He was just like a hunting hound, sniffing after one notion until the scent of another sent him snuffling in a new direction. She took her time walking back along the little path through the barley.

The crows were still keeping away. She looked at the flowers in the hedgerow, trying to remember their names again. It was Dat that had taught Shanco; Martha had never had the chance to learn because she'd always been too busy working. He'd sit in the hedge with him, hiding different flowers behind his back and feeding him a few clues to help him learn the names faster. Her favourite flower was gorse. Nothing manmade could ever capture its yellow, nor its scent! It was exotic, like coconut, like butter: nothing else came close. If she'd ever bought a frock, it would have been a yellow one. She reached the yard and went to the storehouse to lock the door.

Martha froze and cramps gripped her stomach. The screeching was like a pig being slaughtered. She turned around and ran as fast as she could over to the house. She felt Shanco's screams like knives turning inside her. She loved him like a mother. She opened the door and stood stock still.

'What were you up to, you little fucker?'

There was a gun on Jack's shoulder, and it was aimed at Shanco. Judy came out of the parlour, buttoning up her skirt.

'Right little pervert, aren't you?' Judy told Shanco.

'Jack, what're you doing?' Martha asked

'What were *you* doin' is what I wanna know, you fucker!'

'Put that gun down, Jack. I said, put it down!' Shanco was screaming, his eyes wild. He just couldn't catch his breath. He was pressing his chest with one hand and screwing up the cap in the other. 'What's happened? Put that thing down, Jack, will you!'

'He's a daft little dirty fucker! You know what, I'm goin' to kill you!'

'What'd he do then?'

'What d'you think he did? He was watching us like a peepin' fuckin' snoop!'

'Watching what?'

Jack was shaking, the gun still raised. Even Judy wasn't trying to calm him down. Jack came closer to him, bringing the gun right up to his forehead. Shanco screamed louder and fell to his knees.

Martha moved towards Jack but he turned about to face her, and this time aimed the gun at her.

'Jack!' Martha straightened up. Jack's eyes were red and were flitting to and fro between Martha and Shanco. His breathing was heavy and sweat was dripping from his hair. She noticed his flies were undone. 'Jack! What if Mami could see you now?' Slowly her words reached him through the red mist.

'I'd be doin' us all a favour if I topped 'im right now.'

'Come on, Jack, you're scaring him!'

'I'd be doin' us a favour, I tell you; wouldn' 'ave to babysit the little fucker no more then, would we?'

Even Judy had retreated into the pantry.

'J.. jus..'

'Shut your fuckin' trap! Shut it!'

'F... fetchin' the c.. cap,' Shanco said, his eyes closing in fear.

Tears began to stream from Martha's eyes. A wet patch appeared under Shanco's backside.

'Just two of us left then and we've not got long to go anyway.'

The three stood in a triangle, and the only sound was Shanco's tears falling to the floor.

'Jack, just please put that gun away. Mami wouldn't want this! Whatever she did, she wouldn't want this!'

Jack started to breathe more deeply and Martha felt Mami's presence in the triangle. Slowly, as though in a dream, Jack lowered the gun. She noticed that for the first time in years there were tears in her older brother's eyes. He wiped them away roughly with his thumb. He felt his crotch with his left hand and zipped himself up. The wet patch had spread over the lino. Jack moved and felt behind him for somewhere to sit before lowering himself down. His breathing was still heavy and fierce; the sweat had soaked into his collar. Shanco got up quietly, trying to hide the wet under him. He was still holding the cap. He shot out, running for his life. Martha took a cloth and wiped the floor before Judy saw it. Jack watched her, his gaze far away.

'He doesn't understand, Jack.' Martha soaked up the mess, observing her own shaking hands. Jack drew out a hanky and dried his forehead. 'You shouldn't have scared him like that.'

'What was he thinkin' of, watchin' like that?' Jack was rubbing his head. It was getting dark outside.

'That's the way he's always been.'

''E shouldn't 'ave been....'

Martha got up and as she turned caught the faintest smell of cigarettes and the tap of heels going over to Jack. She went outside and called out for Shanco but no answer came, only her own voice echoing back across the empty yard. Bob's kennel was open. Martha went up the lane towards Cae Marged.

As she walked she didn't see how the flowers had started to close. This was the best time of year for flowers, Dat always said. You could see them breathing, see them loll, ready for sleep. All the petals were curling around the centre like lashes round an eye closing against the cold night. There were so many stars this time of year: it seemed as though someone had cast them like quicksilver into the sky. They were welling up like droplets getting ready to fall, hard, to the earth.

Martha turned into Cae Marged. Shanco was there, Bob tight under his jumper, putting the cap on the scarecrow's head. She moved closer to him but Shanco didn't notice. The crows were cawing in the trees close by. Martha watched him staring at the scarecrow as though it were the only thing in the world. The wet patch yawned down the back of his trousers. Shanco stared hard, his eyes dark in the black night. The scarecrow returned a red bleary stare.

TWENTY-FOUR

Shanco wasn't himself for days; his face gone chalky from lack of sleep. Night after night he'd refuse to come into Martha's bed and lay awake like a corpse in Jack's. Silence had settled on him like hoarfrost, and even the present heatwave failed to thaw out his chilly shroud.

The bullocks were let out in a rush of kicking limbs across the fields, and the dapper swallows started to arrive, their chatter filling the yard. One day she heard the cuckoo, and Shanco ran into the house with his hands over his ears to stop himself hearing it properly without there being any pennies in his pocket. As she listened, Martha was reminded of Judy.

First thing, Roy and Jack had been gathering in the sheep. Because Jack had noticed a maggoty sheep, he'd decided to get that year's shearing done early since the weather was so fine. So that she could help later with folding the fleece, Martha had got up early to cook, peeling away the mince from its bag and into the frying pan, letting it spatter and brown. The menu for shearing was always the same: mince, gravy and potatoes, with jelly and custard for pudding. John Penbanc was the shearer; he was a big man with strong arms like a lobster. His reputation was not for being gentle with the animals but he wouldn't dare raise a finger with Jack around. People said he'd driven a nail into the hoof of a bull who was a touch too wild to keep, just so he could claim compensation. The police had come over to his farm suspecting Smokies, blowtorching sheep with their skin on for the people who'd pay to eat that sort of thing. Nothing was proven, though. Jack could handle him anyway.

John always brought his son with him: a tall, thickset boy with hotbaked skin and chest-hair sprouting from his sweaty open collar. He had a wide face and a permanently surprised expression. But he clumped around wildly, as though whoever got in his way might get hit. The scars down his face suggested that sometimes they maybe did, and hit him right back. John always held that he was a good boy, just that trouble seemed to follow once he'd got himself a name as a bruiser. Shanco hated him ever since he'd caught him aiming a sly kick at Bob: he'd keep watch from a distance with Bob stuffed protectively up his jumper.

Jack didn't do the shearing himself any longer because he got so short of breath. And of course he got money on account of his bad back: he didn't want to encourage the gossips. John and his son were glad: Jack could be more of a hindrance lately. These days he'd sit watching the pair at work, making mental notes of any cuts or rough handling.

The trailer had been set up: the lads had a good system in full swing. John's son had made adaptations, after he'd convinced his father, along the lines of his recent shearing experience in New Zealand. By the time Martha reached the field, there were several fleeces waiting for her. Jack was sitting on the fence, waving away insects from his face. The lads had already taken off their shirts and were working in their vests, their feet in moccasins. She always loved the noise and buzz of shearing time, and admired the silent teamwork of the men. She set straight to work on the tarpaulin lain out for her.

Martha took each fleece and pulled out any matted snarls.

107

Then she would shake it out to its full length and fold both sides in, rolling it up tight and tying it into a ball. She worked without a word, cleaning, rolling and then stuffing each one into the corner of the sack of wool hanging on a nearby metal frame. Each year around forty to fifty fleeces fit into a sack. She lost herself in the noise and brightness of the day. Jack watched her quietly. When you considered her age, it was pretty impressive that she could keep up with packing the wool of two fine shearers. He stared at her, his head full of barking, bleating and the purr of the machines. By the time they'd finished with the morning's flock, there was a sheen of lanolin over Martha's arms and clothes. The sound of sheep calling for their lambs was enough to deafen you.

Martha returned to the house to warm the food she had prepared, and to boil the kettle. The heat was unbearable. Jack always insisted they eat outside so that the lads would get straight back to work rather than lazing about. She washed her arms and filled the basket left half-packed on the table. Shanco came to help her, and they carried all they needed together up to the field. Jack went to fetch a bucket, water and a towel for the lads to get washed. John was talking ten to the dozen as usual but his son sat sullenly in the hedge's shadow. The son ate heartily, his huge hands dwarfing the delicate fork. His dubious glances underlined Shanco's odd mannerisms; if Roy came too close to the food, he swore at him. Jack ate his fill too, though he'd done little all morning.

'It was up Llain, I was, you know,' John was in full flow. 'She'd brought us a big pot of soup up the field; left it by the hedge. Round the corner I come; some little bitch had knocked the lid off and gone head over heels into the fuckin'

108

thing. I'm telling you, the dog was dripping with the stuff! Got hold of her collar, I did; let the soup drip back into the saucepan. I did, you know. No need to let things go waste, is there? Definite. You know what? Not a drop was left. Tasted no fuckin' different!'

Jack smiled. John's son mopped up gravy with his bread regardless; the story was part of a well-tried repertoire. Shanco's eyes widened, sensing how Bob would feel up to his neck in soup. He gripped him harder. The breeze was light, shifting a dappled shadow through the leaves onto the little picnic party. The bullocks had gathered nosily the other side of the hedge, jostling to get a glimpse over, and twitching their tails now and then. Bob cocked his head whenever he caught sight of them. The strengthening sun beat hard on their heads.

'Hear about Hirnant, did you?' Silence. 'Son gone off to Australia. Met some woman out there and never came back, so they say. Old man'll have to give up milking now. Was in a pretty bad shape to kick off with.'

Jack stirred his third sugar into his tea, the news sinking into him slowly. This was how they kept up with the world outside: just let their visitors tell their story. They hardly ever went anywhere, nor talked to anyone, and yet news would usually reach them somehow all the same. Having to eat his mince and keep Bob under his jumper was one job too many for Shanco to be able to sit comfortably. As the party finished their meal, Martha took out some bowls from the basket. The custard was in a plastic bottle which she squeezed, sharing out five portions. She opened an old ice cream carton full of jelly gone runny in the heat. She doled it all out carefully then threw a spoon towards each diner.

John Penbanc's store of stories was shared out fairly too, but the best he kept until last.

'That's it, then…. What about that Gwynfor, then; heard he used to be a regular round here. Gone and got married, he has, in the registry office, so they say.' Martha let go of her spoon, spilling jelly all down her apron. Shanco stared at her, his spoon still in his mouth. 'Lot younger than him, no one could believe it. She's from round Lampeter way, that's it. So they say.' The insects hung over the food like a veil. 'Heard they'd had to tie the knot, know what I mean. Jack shouted over to Roy, who was barking at a lamb. Roy dropped to the floor. John studied Martha's face, winked, and went on, 'Who'd have thought, eh, the dirty old dog! That's the way it goes.'

John wasn't born a cruel man; his habit of stirring things up had been fed by hard work and circumstances. He couldn't resist the temptation, and, given the chance, he'd add his pennyworth then take a back seat to enjoy the show. His wife used to tell him off, but she had got used to it; his son, meanwhile, just got angry in defence. The breeze grew stronger.

'And how's your ladyfriend then, Jack?'

'Back to work then,' Jack replied. John and Martha glanced at him, the former pleased he seemed to have struck a nerve, Martha thinking Jack must have come to her rescue. Jack, though, just felt the afternoon's work and evening milking pressing. She packed the food with trembling hands and set the basket under the hedge.

The news had thrown Martha; she was glad to distract herself with physical work. She threw herself into wrapping up each fleece, the noise around her a comfort. The sun's heat and bright light had given her a headache. She wasn't actually too keen on this time of year. The bushes were too green, the goldenchain bright yellow and there were too many flowers. Sometimes its energy just seemed to sap her. Whenever she walked out in the evening, she'd feel overwhelmed by the lambs' bleating and swallows' chatter, the green growth's stifling breath. She was relieved when teatime came and she escaped back to the cool darkness of the house to boil the kettle once again. Her vision was a blue blur before she adjusted to the house's shade. She filled the flasks, grabbed a handful of teabags and set off back towards the field. They could use the same cups.

By the end of the day the holding pens were nearly empty, the earth churned up brown with even hoof marks. A maggoty store lamb and sheep had been left behind. The field had about it the frenzy of a fairground: sheep calling for their lambs, the contractors packing up. Martha watched the sheep spreading out, their cropped wool unbearably bright. One or two had lurid purple salve squirted onto a cut. John and his son left without a word about money. The bill would arrive as ever; they had their sights on the next farm and setting up their stall there for the morning. John's son put up his feet on the Land Rover's dashboard; John was already thinking of his tea. His jibes about Gwynfor were far from his mind: that's the sort of man he was, jab in his lance and leave the wounded get on with it.

'Come on then, let's get this over with.'

Jack lifted up his leg stiffy over the little gate to corner the remaining sheep. Its wool was wet where the maggots had eaten its flesh. He threw a bowlful of Jeyes Fluid over the wound and the three watched the liquid turn milky as it soaked into the wool. Then the swelling maggots surfaced, flinching through the skin and falling to the ground in one heap. The ewe took a deep breath, looking over its shoulder to where it felt itching as the maggots left.

111

The lamb with a stinking wound on its back was last. Jack had found it in the woods, and even though he wasn't sure it was one of theirs, he'd decided to keep it as part-payment for the three pet lambs lost last year. There was a hole in the lamb's back; you could see the maggots moving under the skin like water coming to the boil. This one was unlikely to last the week untreated. Jack poured on the liquid and the lamb bucked as it burnt into it. Shanco held harder onto its neck and pressed it against the side of the pen, the wire imprinting a grid on its wool. The bullocks were still enjoying the show from over the hedge. The maggots churned away but were in too deep to get out. They'd have to be extracted by hand. Jack hooked a finger far into the hole and flicked the maggots out of the wet flesh so they fell to the ground in a white rain. Shanco shut his eyes tight; Martha wrinkled her nose. The smell of rotting flesh and the harsh liquid making her reel a little in this heat, she steadied herself against the side of the pen. Jack poured more fluid into the empty wound and let the lamb go. The three watched it as it went, its hindquarters quivering. Martha felt the pain it must have suffered, and its relief.

'Well, the fucker'll either die of shock or be fit by the weekend.'

Jack wiped his fingers in his trousers and set off over to the milking parlour. Shanco picked up the tins and the syringes, and put them into the food basket. He walked towards the storehouse, still holding Bob tight. Martha waited a while, watching the lamb struggling across the field, its head twitching.

TWENTY-FIVE

That night after tea, Martha went to sit on the pink sofa in the parlour. It was cold in there, quiet and dark; it was a refuge for her from the day. She tried to knead cool comfort into her raw shoulders. She felt as though she'd been flailed. You could hear Jack and Shanco moving in the kitchen and Jack's voice rumbling at Bob.

A hot sunset sent amber fingers through the window. It was like a magnifying glass that intensified dark and light, and all the colours in between. Martha sank deeper into the sofa's cool velvet. She heard chairs scraping as the men left and went out into the fields to see if the hay was ready to harvest.

Martha's back ached; she felt like a wet rag. She nursed her cup while her arm muscles burned. She had changed out of her work-clothes before coming in here, but the lanolin still shone on her arms, anointing her, making her skin young and healthy. The light stealthily sought her out.

She was lit up like an insect in amber. It was as though the beauty of her fresh skin was on display; the soft lines of her face, the depth of her brown eyes. The light found rich colours in her dark hair. She looked for a moment almost like an icon. Dat used to say she was like a dolly, though. And on the pink sofa, in the yellow light, you could see that fragility about her too.

You could feel the still of that cool room like heat. As the light faded, shapes and colours revealed themselves for the first time. The piano was shining black with low red lights, like a horse's hide. Martha stared at it, her eyes moist.

She hadn't ever played it. Hadn't even pressed down a note, aside from the chords you strike when dusting, which she did each week with devotion. She felt that since she'd never learnt, she had no right to play. Now and then she'd get out the books from the stool; look at the music. The notes looked like those crows outside on the powerline. She let her eyes run over the treble clef, its sinuous curves. She kept the lid shut only to keep Shanco out; she knew Jack couldn't care less.

Martha looked at the carpet where she'd wiped up Gwynfor's spilt tea from that time. The stain was pretty much gone. She thought of his footprints in the garden. She set down her cup and placed her hand into her apron pocket where she kept the piano key. The crafted curve of the metal felt delicate in her heavy fingers as she got up. By this time, the sun was low. The piano stool was velvet too; she touched it before sitting down. The two frail arms of the seat fitted around her frame. She put the fancy key in the lock and turned: it opened with a relieved click. Martha took a deep breath and raised the lid slowly, her hands shaking. The piano's smile was wide, giving her a straight choice, in black and white, to let its keys open a few new doors for her. She yielded to the temptation of touching one: there was coolness in the smooth ivory; and promise. She shut her eyes and pressed it. She was startled as the soundwaves disturbed the thick air. It was an ugly note, a wrong one, a crow's caw. Martha started crying, her tears on the cold ivory like a gentle drumbeat.

Martha didn't realise, but you shouldn't have a piano against a damp wall like the pantry, used for generations to salt pork. Salt and damp from the wall had been seeping into the back of the piano for months, its insides swelling, distorting the sound. The house had simply killed the piano.

The light was weak now, as Martha's tears salted the piano keys in the after-echo of that ugly note. That amber light held her a while in its warm embrace, then left her alone in darkness.

Jack and Shanco had been checking the hay and barley fields before their last job. The cattle was grazing in strips at this time of year, to eke out their feed: Jack and Shanco would move the electric fence each night so they could move onto fresh grass. Jack used to have a remote-controlled collar for punishing misbehaving sheepdogs when he was training them. Shanco had been scared of anything to do with electricity ever since Jack had put the collar on him and threatened to press the button. Jack had been tempted to use it on Bob to stop him killing the kittens, but reckoned at least it saved him drowning the buggers. Either way they were gonners.

You could hear the electric wire ticking loudly tonight. The cattle were gazing eagerly at the green grass on the other side.

'Go on, touch it.'

'N... no.'

'Come on.'

'N.. n... *no*!'

''God's sake, don't be a baby!' Shanco stubbornly shoved his hands into his pockets. 'I'll tell Martha you're a Mummy's Boy,' Jack knew which buttons to press to make Shanco jump, all right. 'Tell you what,' He looked around for nettles and grabbed a tall one. He lent down, cut it at the stem and plucked off each leaf. Jack must be so brave to do that, Shanco thought. Truth was Jack's hands were so hard he hardly felt anything, and in any case he had an old trick of picking the leaves from underneath, where the poison was weakest. 'Go on, touch it with this: you won't feel a thing!'

Shanco worked out that the length of the nettle would put a bit of distance between him and the electric shock, and anyway he could be just as brave as Jack. He took the stem and moved closer to the fence. He listened to the electric hissing. He touched the wire with the stem and waited. Nothing. He turned to smile at Jack and wham! The shock hit him, twice as hard for having travelled first along the plant-stem. Shanco let go of it, feeling the pain in his chest.

'Ow!!!' he shouted, frightening the cattle away across the field. Jack was creased up laughing, watching him jump up and down with his hand between his knees. Bob was barking away in sympathy. Jack knew Shanco wasn't in any real danger, that the whole thing would be forgotten by morning. He went into a big sulk though, walking half a field's breadth behind Jack as they returned to the yard. When they got there, they found themselves in darkness, the sun's last light having faded over the side of the house.

TWENTY-SIX

'M... M... Martha.'

Martha opened her eyes and saw Shanco's face inches above hers. His expression was dark. She moved over and shifted the bolster down the middle of the bed as usual. His need for sleep and the stink in his own room must have driven him in here. In a box under his bed were the corpses of a rabbit and a magpie Shanco had found in the garden. They'd been there days but he'd brought them in anyway and carried them upstairs in a box. Now the smell would knock you flat. He had managed to keep her out of his room for a few weeks by pushing a chair under the doorknob, going back and forth to Cae Berllan the meanwhile through the window. He'd have to get rid of them tomorrow.

Shanco made the most of the heat Martha's body had left on the blanket. He closed his eyes and waited: usually he'd be asleep within minutes of being there. She had recently got used to sleeping on her own: if Shanco's reappearance was going to be a regular thing, she'd have to readjust all over again. She kept her eyes closed but every nerve was on alert. Shanco's breathing had regained its rhythm after his trip across the landing, but he was just as wide awake as she was. They both lay there resting; hardly breathing, aware of the other's being conscious, but each skull a bird cage full of thoughts flapping in the hope of freedom.

Martha thought about where Gwynfor would be sleeping tonight. Might be over with that woman, could be she'd moved in with him by now. News would reach her somehow, someday. Amazing she'd taken so long to find out; that's what happens when you miss a few trips to town. Not his fault anyway, she thought: Martha'd made her bed and she'd lie on it. Thoughts came to mind of John Penbanc's loose tongue at shearing; of how soon shearing time would come around again; also, of the barley in the field. Sometimes, close to sleep, the field would be before her in broad daylight: the green fuse of barley, the wind rustling the ears into waves of shallow water. Nausea came with the waves and she thought of Judy.

Jack had been spending more time over there with her lately. Sometimes he was even late for milking. One morning she and Shanco'd had to start doing it on their own. He stank of beer, he did, a stink that'd lasted till morning. They said Judy liked a tipple: looked like he was following in her stiletto footsteps pretty sharpish.

Shanco liked to keep the scarecrow company of an evening, out in the barley field: he was thinking about him now. Bound to be scared, poor scarecrow. He thought of those animals in the box, how young and healthy they'd seemed, and how strange it was to have found them yards apart from each other: all dead. He closed his eyes to shut out the image of what he'd seen in the parlour: Jack and Judy on top of one another. He couldn't think about that with Martha lying so close: after all, she might be able to see into his head. Shanco thought of Bob. He'd caught quite a few rabbits lately, and a rat, but he'd no interest in those animals in the garden, for they were dead already. The enjoyment Bob got out of his prey was to run after them and worry them, not eat them.

Martha opened her eyes; Shanco opened his. They lay

there, witness to the waning half-light. She turned towards him, but he took no notice. His face was angular, wan. Her eyes caressed it, drawing up into her own eyes the moisture welling in his. She wondered whether he might be awake after all. He knew how to sleep with his eyes open; she'd seen him do it when he was younger. She remembered how Jack would call it unnatural, like a horse sleeping on its feet. She turned back towards the window. The sky had penned in white clouds above the fields; morning mist was washing over the yard. She felt jealous: she'd like a wash and brush up like that each day, a new start.

Martha must have dozed off in the early hours, because she didn't hear Shanco getting up. He went across the landing and into his room, pulled on his trousers over his Long Johns, and hooked his braces onto his shoulders. He put on a shirt and jumper. He went down on his knees to fish out the box and put it on the bed. As he pulled on his socks he couldn't resist taking a peek. He lifted up the corner but the smell was unbearable: a mixture of feather and fur all matted together. He let the lid drop.

Shanco had been one to hoard bits and pieces and move them about the house since he was a little boy. Maybe his love of hiding things came from always being the last to understand anything: when it came to his own special things, he was the only one who knew where they were.

He went to the bottom drawer of his bedside cupboard and slowly opened it. Here were his treasures; his world hidden in a hanky. Martha's necklace, the one she thought she'd lost. Jack's key. Judy's hair bobble. He picked up one of his latest acquisitions and put it in his pocket. He closed the drawer.

Shanco stood and picked up the box. It wouldn't be long before he'd have to feed the calves. He took the box downstairs, stroking the new treasure in his pocket. A little white bottle with a label on it and a yellow cap like a crown of hair.

TWENTY-SEVEN

Jack had borrowed Will's harvester and within a morning, several acres had been cut. Jack then spent half the week turning the hay over and gathering it up into rows as light and dry as kindling, ready for baling. Jack felt he was a dab hand at this part of the harvest. This morning he was walking the rows, evening out any clumps of hay that could choke the machine. Sometimes he'd stoop to lift a whole armful, as if it were some wayward scarecrow child, and dump it further down the line. This way he knew the rows would hold no surprises, like they had one year when he'd had to pay through the nose to mend a machine wrecked by some bits of metal in among the hay. He reckoned someone had done it deliberately, to get back at him for some slight or other.

Jack walked slowly, bending down once or twice to pick up and throw into the hedge an animal corpse caught and crushed by the machine's blades. It was too early for baling: you had to wait for the sun to burn off the dew. The pasture where it had been cut between the rows looked bright and new, like clean shorn sheep. This was his favourite time of year and his favourite job. Anyone could make silage: this year's showground with its contractors' shouts and loud machinery had already come and gone. Gathering the hay was special.

Years ago, they'd had an army of helpers. Now though, all their neighbours were as old as they were. Since there were no children on the farm, they didn't know the local young men. Will used to get sent over by his mother. There was also Dai One Eye, and Tommy, who, despite the fact that he'd lost his legs in the war, used to drive that old van Dat had bought. He'd follow the lads around the fields, the van's headlamps lighting up the scene when the work went on late. With some old coats under his backside and two long brushes under his armpits, he was a driver to match the best. These days, with no one to help, you just had to cut a little at a time.

Martha had got up early; she and Shanco were getting dinner in a basket ready. Jack usually started baling round about half ten; then they would both have to go up to the field to stack the bales, collect and bring them into the haybarn. Shanco was at the kitchen table shelling boiled eggs; Martha was making up cheese and tomato sandwiches. He watched her as she closed down each sandwich. If she caught him looking, she'd make a show for him with the bread slices, opening and closing them as though they were talking. He loved it, and also the prospect of ginger beer which he knew was close, because he'd seen yeast frothing in bowls a few days ago. She was trying to make up to him after she'd given him the third degree about a dead old magpie and rabbit she'd found earlier, down the bottom of the garden.

Harvest was a special time for Shanco too, because he knew how well he could stack and carry, easily clearing half the field on his own. Despite being so thin, he was strong. 'Spider silk's stronger than steel,' Mami'd always say about Shanco. Bob loved chasing mice in and out of the overgrown hedges. Strangely enough, the same as at shearing and any other day they could really use some help, Judy had found some expedition to go on that couldn't do without her, 'sorry about that'.

Martha drew a teatowel over the basket and walked with Shanco over to the field. The sun was already bright, throwing light like a knife to the earth. The shorn pasture on their way bristled against her ankles. She set down the basket by the bottom hedge and they both set to work digging their fingers under the twine and carrying the bales together into a pile which they stacked in short columns. Because Jack had dried the hay so well, most of the bales, apart from those in the furthest, wettest, corner were light. He'd finished baling by now and, while the others weren't looking, went to lift those heavier ones. Martha had noticed Jack was quieter lately, seemed driven, somehow. Madame hadn't been around so often; mind you, he still spent every night over there.

The sun was above them now: without a word being given, they all gathered to eat. The three sat, backs against one stack, its shadow a balm. Martha opened the basket. The hay had scratched the soft white underpart of their forearms. Across their palms were deep cane-strokes seared by the twine. They ate quietly, Jack throwing a crust now and again to Bob, and making Shanco wonder why he was being so nice.

By mid afternoon it had all been stacked, so Jack went to do the milking. When that was done, the calves had been fed and they'd eaten a quick tea, they went back out to the hay. Jack drove the tractor while the others bounced away on the trailer and Bob barked from under Shanco's jumper. Martha stood on the trailer in the field, taking the bales that were handed up to her. Then Jack would park the tractor again a little further on. The gnats were out, and were making a meal of Shanco especially, making him dance like he was on knives. Martha and Jack enjoyed the show.

As darkness fell, they needed the tractor headlamps: its rays fell across the stubble. They took a break for tea and watched the moths' five seconds of limelight. Some of them lasted longer though, and Shanco smiled to see how they came back for more punishment after knocking against the lamps time and again. How pretty they were, all cream and brown colours, their soft fuzz, their false livery of black eyes painted on wings. No one ever noticed them during the day.

The field cleared, Jack drove the tractor over to the haybarn, the other two perched high on the load. As they followed the hedgerows, the topmost branches brushed over them: Shanco lay on his back, letting the cool broad leaves flap at him.

Martha went to fetch the old tractor to light up the haybarn. She put on a heavy jumper and threw one across to Shanco. The elevator was set up and they started to unload. Jack was in the thick of it, a strange sight with a white mask across his mouth. She smiled. This job was the only one for which Jack wore any sort of safety gear. This white tortoise across his chin was his shield against the dust rising from the old hay underfoot. As a little boy he'd listened to Dat's coughing, and had been scared silly of getting Farmer's Lung ever since. Martha had opened her room onto the landing once to see little Jack crouched down, face pressed between the banisters. He'd been listening, tears streaming, to Dat's last coughs. For one whole year he'd kept Dat's hanky under his jumper. He was still only a little blond boy in short trousers, but on the day Jack did the milking on his own for the first time, she saw him burn that hanky on the kitchen fire.

Half past midnight and the trailer was empty, leaving only wisps like stray hairs on the wooden boards. The barn was filling up. Grass-seed and sweat stuck to their skin. It was quiet at last. Martha stood for a second listening to the high pitch of bats, watching Jack wipe his face with a hanky, the mask a communion cup hovering beneath his face. Bob scrambled into Shanco's arms and he threw Bob lightly into his kennel. Shanco looked around. He was tired, but he couldn't sleep yet. He paused a second then walked towards Cae Marged to see the barley. In the darkness it was silver like the sea. He walked over to the scarecrow, a figure in shadow on a cross. The barley ran between his fingers like sand at the seaside. The moon was like a big headlamp shining in on him. The scarecrow looked sicklier than ever, Shanco thought. He wished him Good Night and turned slowly back to the house.

TWENTY-EIGHT

'Aberaeron mackerel!'

Sam Fish's cry was loud as the bell on his boat. Just a few weeks in the summer, before the seagulls turned seawards, his cries of fish rang around the local farmyards. '*Aberaeron* mackerel!' He opened the back of the van and pulled towards him his weighing scales, the bundle of newspaper for wrapping and his knife. He caught sight of Shanco, peeping, behind him, and turned to face him. '*Aberaeron* mackerel!'

Shanco closed his eyes as the streetcry's full force hit him. 'How are you, lad? Didn't see you there,' Sam said, smiling. A fag was stuck between two gappy top teeth, the only ones left in the row. 'Where's that fuckin' dog of yours today, then? Locked away, he'd better be, or I'll slice open his belly with this knife!'

Last time he'd called, Bob had jumped into the van through the driver's window and sneaked in among the fish boxes. He'd had a whole Friday of fish by the time Sam had finished his story about the fuckin' Spaniards hooverin' up fish out of the sea, and then them buggers from Brussels and the EU or whatever the wasters called themselves, puttin' the fisherman out of business.

Sam threw away his fag and squashed it underfoot. He had a chubby red face and a big red nose. In the summer, sea and sun made his cheeks redden like apples, the blackheads around his nose as plain as small stones on yellow sand. His flabby neck was scored with V-shaped lines

126

like distant birds. He always wore the same brown trousers, wellingtons and white vest. He rubbed his stomach and smiled at Shanco. Martha appeared.

'*Aber-*,' Sam began.

'Alright, alright!' she interrupted.

'How do, how do, Matilda? Well, don't you look pretty today! Going on a trip?' She had her hair in pink sponge curlers and her purse was out ready. But she wasn't smiling, not at all. When Sam first used to call, she'd correct his 'Matilda'. But five years in, she'd realised it made no difference. Still, she'd also realised Judy had got called Matilda once, when she'd happened to be out in the yard, so it can't have been personal, just his way round learning his customers' names. 'How much today then, Missus? I reckon you're a bit hungry. This lad 'ere can pack 'em away inside for you, I bet.' He put a friendly hand on Shanco's shoulder, his knife waving.

Shanco was hypnotised by the sight, in the back of the old Ford van, of stacked boxes full of fish like stripy silver tigers, lighting up the dark interior. These creatures, each somehow the same and yet with their own stamp like our fingerprints, seemed to him from another strange and salty world.

'Six today; thanking you.'

'Remember this is a growing lad,' Sam winked, pushing his luck.

'Just six, thank you.'

'Six big ones then.'

'No. Six of the usual size. They taste better than the big ones.'

'Right-oh, six it is then,' Sam replied, fumbling among the fishy mix behind him. He chose six and put them on the scales. 'Here we go, then, just over six pounds here.'

'I'm sure you meant to clean them before weighing them, Sam.'

'Well, well, you drive a hard bargain and no mistake,' he said with a theatrical sigh, 'Catch me out every time, you do.' A wink for Martha this time.

Sam sold them whole as a rule, but for some reason for Martha – could it be her serene face? – he'd usually clean them before weighing so she'd get better value for money. As a rule she got an extra one for luck as well.

They watched Sam slicing through the hard skin so that the pink guts oozed out. He cut off their heads and ran the flat of the blade down each backbone to cut away the cord of blood that spoiled the taste. As it touched each bone the knife gave a small metallic click like clockwork. He weighed them again and wrapped them in newspaper. Martha dropped the money into his bloody, slimy hand, sequinned with silver scales.

'Many thanks then, Matilda!'

He flung the money into an ice cream carton, scraped the pile of guts into another sheet and gave it to Shanco for the cat. The rest he slung into the van, and slamming the door, he jumped into the front and drove off on a dustwave, shouting, 'See you next year then, if I'm not in Davy Jones' locker!'

They stood in his wake, each holding their strange packages.

Mami'd never let any mackerel near the place. No better than a rat, she said it was, eating anything, even dead stuff, off the seafloor.

Martha set them on their backs in the oven with a sprinkle of salt over the light-coloured flesh. She started cutting thick slices of white bread and put them in the basket on the table. She got Shanco to open the windows to let the smell out. Jack was getting washed. At least being with Judy meant he washed properly, not like the lick and promise he used to treat himself to. She realised she hadn't seen Judy for quite a while. According to Jack, she was away 'sorting out stuff to do with the divorce'.

Martha had threatened Shanco with him and Bob missing the picnic unless he washed, and he'd let her run a flannel over him that morning. When he was little, Mami'd make him stand on a stool to get washed with a flannel and a basin of hot water, since he was scared of the deep bath water. Nowadays he would sit while Martha washed his upper body, scouring the skin until it shone red. She'd let him wash his bottom half then, while he glanced around wildly to check her back was turned. Right now he was sitting on the settle, wearing a clean jumper, his usual waxy complexion rubbed red raw. She had even persuaded him to let her wash his green woolly cap: it was drooping on a peg over the stove as though it had taken offence.

While the mackerel was cooking, Martha took out her curlers, ran her fingers through her hair and took off her apron. Jack came into the kitchen and sat sullenly on the settle. He'd even shaved. Martha opened the stove and the room filled with the sharp salt smell of seaside, sun and summer. Martha pulled the six portions by their tails onto a plate. She covered them in foil and filled a flask with tea. When it was all ready, Shanco and Jack followed Martha out through the back door.

As they did each year, the three walked up the lane, Shanco following a way behind, Martha carrying the basket. Jack was breathless and was moving slower than usual. They went past Cae Marged and Macyn Poced, straight up to

Banc Ucha, where the view was best. The three had come here every year since they could remember, first of all with Mami and Dat. It was tradition by now too that Jack would grumble about having to take the afternoon off, since lazing about was not in his nature. This year, though, he came like a lamb.

They sat on the hillside with the whole valley at their feet. It was hot and insects rose in a cloud around the blanket as Martha spread it out. As they sat down, Bob ran away into a nearby bush. After their meal, Shanco lay down and tried to measure the clouds with his fingers. The others stayed quiet.

Beneath them was the town, busy on the Bank Holiday. Behind them was the village church; you could faintly hear children playing around the square. There was a lawnmower in the distance, and insects hovering against a dappled leafy backdrop. For all of them, this was the only afternoon off they had all year, if you didn't count the evening milking. Jack sat stiffly in his clean trousers.

'Llain's a bit late with the 'arvest,' he noticed.

Shanco carried on his measurements and added to the equation how many birds were in the air.

Martha's fingers were greasy; she sat there fussily so that her hands wouldn't dirty her loose trousers. She quietly cursed herself for forgetting to pack her apron. It was getting hotter. Jack plucked at his collar.

'It's nice here, isn't it?' she said. In the distance, the sea was one strip, like the striplight in the milking parlour. She looked back at the graveyard. 'Remember that day one of the Jehova's Witnesses came round and Mami was in the middle of painting the stairs?' Jack was waving an insect out of his eyes. 'He told her the world would be ending that week,' Jack's smile spread slowly, 'and Mami told him, "Then why am I bothering to paint these flippin' stairs?"'

Jack laughed quietly. Shanco smiled, not wanting to be left out. Martha fiddled with the grass at the corner of the blanket and watched a spider trying to climb up onto it. Jack's head was starting to get hot.

'And the day everyone came around to help with the 'ay,' Jack began, Martha smiling, 'and Mami'd made sandwiches for us the night before. Out we go into the fields and when it's dinner time we all pile into the sandwiches. Except all there was left, was bread! His nibs over 'ere only got up in the middle of the night and ate the ham out of every damn one of 'em!' Shanco sat up and smiled, his interest in the clouds suddenly waning. Martha pulled an ivy leaf from a nearby tree and studied it. It was smooth, cold, as big as her hand. Mami used to make her trace with a needle each vein on an ivy leaf when she was learning to sew, make her puncture her progress. If she was wide of the mark, she'd get her ears boxed. In the end, though, Mami's hands were a bit like this leaf: her veins punctured by needles. Martha threw away the leaf. 'And the time this one 'ere started wanderin' about in the middle of the night! Came upstairs and I shouted out, "Shanco! Is that you?" Didn't want to answer, did 'e, so 'e barked like a dog instead; I said, "Oh it's you, Bob, is it?" Idiot answered, "Yes," didn't 'e!'

Jack was shaking with laughter; Martha couldn't stop herself either when she saw Jack's young laughing face. Shanco followed suit, and Bob reappeared, his tail held straight up in the air, showing his surprise.

Jack took a deep breath, 'Where'd it all go, eh?' The question hung high in the air, like heat haze above the town. Martha's smile slowly straightened and she stared ahead, still trying to think of an answer. 'Right then,' Jack said, wiping his hands on his trousers, 'Better get movin'. Another year of work to get on with.'

She packed it all away and the three walked towards the house, Bob barking after them. The Bank Holiday could get along without them.

TWENTY-NINE

'Where'd that calf go then? It's been born, I know it 'as.'

Jack came in, flushed, for breakfast. Shanco came in behind him, his face lit up with a grin.

'What's the matter now then, Jack?'

'Fuckin' cow's had 'er calf and gone and 'idden it.'

Shanco laughed but then Jack's glance was enough to wither a rose.

'You sure it's come?'

'Course I'm fuckin' sure, woman! She looked like she was dilating last night, and her waters and the afterbirth were out there.'

'Oh.'

'I'll give you bloody "Oh"!'

'And you've looked all over the field?'

'What d'you fuckin' think I've been doin'?'

Jack sat down irritably at the table. Even though the hay was safe in the barn and they were going to harvest the barley today, something was eating Jack. The cow had simply chosen the wrong day to hide her calf. They did it now and then, God only knows why. They did it so well sometimes, days could go by before they found it. And it wasn't a trick they learnt in response to bad experience: some cows did it with their first calf.

Martha brought the plates over to the table. 'We'll have to walk round every inch of that field, in case she's got out somewhere.'

Shanco ate quietly. It was such an adventure: going out on the trail of something nobody had ever seen.

'Did the old bitch 'ave to do it on the day we want the barley in?'

It was a fine day, the sun had a tinge of autumn. Shanco's face was brown; his nose pink; when Martha rolled up her sleeves you could see the sun's tidemark. She'd given the house a good cleaning yesterday, leaving all the windows open overnight. Mami'd always done this after the lambing, the hay harvest and most of the hard work was over. It was a farewell, in a way, to a year's work, and a welcome to the barley harvest and the autumn. The bedclothes she'd washed and aired; the windows she'd polished and even the piano.

'Shanco and me'll go and look for the calf now; you just get on with the barley.'

Jack looked at her without a word. Leaving anything for anyone else to do didn't come easily to him. But pressure of time made his mind up. He had his vest on, his customary check shirt abandoned, so it must have been hot. The vest stretched tight across his middle, the sweat he'd worked up from milking had made a wet patch on his chest. His mug was pushed roughly to one side as he got up and went out, his mind elsewhere as always at harvest.

Shanco stayed to help Martha wash the dishes; letting them drip-dry in the warm room. She made herself a headscarf from a hanky and they headed out to hunt for the calf.

The pair leaned against the gate to the field where the cow was grazing, her udder full and thickly veined. There was no doubt she had calved. They could wait for the calf to come and feed, but that could take ages and Jack needed their help, so they went into the field and started walking

134

the hedgerows. A cow is a highly defensive animal, so her reactions were some sort of guide to how close they were to her calf. Jack had been hit by a cow one year: he was amazed how a milky, mild Friesian could turn nasty if pushed.

They walked slowly, keeping one eye on the cow, but she stayed put. They walked right round the field, peering into the hedges and stirring them up with a stick. Martha could imagine the calf sunbathing safe with its mother close by, green grass framing its fresh pale form, all oversized ears and eyelashes. No sign though. They walked around the field the other way, looking just as hard again. Shanco scratched his head.

'Come on, we'll have a look on the other side. Maybe it's got out somehow.' The pair stared into the far side of the hedges and shouted their way around them, hoping to startle the creature out of its hiding place. No luck. She knew they'd spent a good part of the morning by now, and Jack would be waiting for them. 'Come on, we'll have to leave it for now; we'll come back tonight.'

Warming to the adventure, Shanco insisted on walking round one final time. He'd set his heart on being the first, on calling out to Martha, on claiming fame as the calf finder.

'Come on.'

Shanco's stick, stirring in the undergrowth, was by now going through the motions. Head down, he followed her over to the yard. She noticed how quiet it was. The pair listened to the birds singing. Roy was scratching and whimpering to be let out of his kennel. Shanco let Bob go so he could follow.

They walked from the yard to Cae Marged, Shanco's disappointment forgotten. He was naming the flowers in the hedges again; Martha listened. They turned into the field. The barley was a fine sight: even, yellow waves in the slight breeze. The pair looked around them. The machine was at the corner ready, but there was no sign of Jack. The oak was thick with crows; above the thicket of trees, more waited.

Heat rose from the earth: a sweet warm scent filled their nostrils. Bob was nosing in the barley already.

'Must be in the house,' Martha said, going over to the machine. She went around the edge of the field, to avoid trampling the barley just before it was brought in. Shanco set out to look for Bob who had run off somewhere and was barking away, worrying some poor creature.

Martha looked at the machine which had heated up in the sun. She reached to touch the scorching metal, drew away. This must be the hottest day of the year.

'M... Martha!'

She looked up and saw Shanco running towards her full pelt. The barley was scattered all ways.

'Watch the barley, you idiot!'

'M... Martha!' He stayed where he was to avoid trampling on the barley. He looked down and pointed at the scarecrow in the middle of the field. 'J... Jack's....'

She saw that Shanco was crying. She ran towards Bob who was barking over by the scarecrow. Shanco ran ahead of her.

At the foot of the scarecrow, Jack was lying with his eyes closed. His face was red and it was blue. Martha fell to her knees.

'Jack... Jack... say something.' She pulled at his vest. 'Jack....' She put her head on his chest to see if he was breathing. She listened, with Shanco above her, fingering his trousers and shifting from one foot to the other. 'He's still breathing, but not much, not enough! Jack! Jack! I'm going to... going to phone someone!'

She looked back over to the house. She couldn't send Shanco, even though he could run faster than her. She took off her headscarf and put it over Jack's face as shelter from the sun.

'S... stay here now, OK, Shanco?' He looked like he'd rather run away. 'You stay here and don't you leave him for a second.' Shanco nodded. 'I won't be long.'

Martha got up and ran as fast as she could right through the barley, towards the house. There was no sign of a car there, as Judy had taken the 4x4 to town and wouldn't be back for ages. The only other option was to phone an ambulance, but that could take hours to get here. She thought of phoning Will or Gwynfor. She reached the house, ran to the old phone in the passage and dialled the number with trembling hands.

'Ambulance please: quickly!' The operator seemed far away, her English speech making her sound further still. 'It's my brother, yes. He's fallen over in the field. Graig-ddu...'

'Gr... can you repeat that?'

'Yes, Graig-ddu. There's no house number, no. G... R.. um.. A... for apple, yes; I...' She thought she heard the woman typing. 'It's not in a town, no. The nearest village is Llanmydr. L... L.. A... N.. Please have you got anyone who speaks Welsh?

'Well, you'll have to come to the village; then once you've passed the church you have to turn left. But that's the church; don't turn left by the chapel or you'll get lost. Follow that road for two miles and then you've got a fork in the road.. yes, a fork... and you've got to take the right lane.'

The panic was tightening Martha's chest. 'Are they on their way? Sorry, yes, please; he's very ill. Yes, take the right lane and then carry on that one for a hundred yards. Then it's the second lane on the left. You can't miss it. No... there's no sign at the top of the lane but I'll send my little brother to stand there... I'll send my little brother to stand there so you know it's the right place. Mobile? No... I don't think I've got one. Yes. Thank you very much.'

Martha set the phone down and went to fetch a cloth and run it under the cold tap. She ran back to the field and placed it over Jack's forehead. He was just as ill as when she left him; Shanco was sitting at the scarecrow's feet, looking at Jack with tears streaming.

'Go and stand at the top of the lane, Shanco, so's the ambulance men'll know they're in the right place. Go and stay there; don't move until they've got here. I've told them you'll be there. And bring them straight here.'

He got up, eager to help. He ran as fast as Roy would to the top of the lane. Martha watched him go and put Jack's head gently in her lap. The quiet had closed around them again; Jack's breath was getting fainter and fainter. She looked around her. He must have been lying there long enough for the barley to have got squashed underneath him, suggesting he'd been conscious a while after collapsing. She laid a hand on him, trying to feel the heartbeats. They came softly like a light rain. The wind whispered through the barley as the crows got closer. Jack's lips were blue and dry; there was some strange cast across his cheeks. Martha held his head in her lap, her hand still pressed to his heart. The sun had shifted round, throwing the shadow of a cross across the pair.

Far beyond the village, the ambulance was lost, the driver

having had to check and check again the name with headquarters, who didn't know the area either. They were looking for a remote farm with a small boy sent to stand at the top of the lane.

THIRTY

By the time the ambulance got there and worked out what Shanco was stammering, Jack's breathing had grown weaker. Martha had been crying so much, her front was all wet. The ambulance couldn't get closer than the gate to the field, so Jack was carried away across it like a corpse. She ran to the house to fetch a cardigan and her purse, and she came back out to go along with him. Shanco followed her into the house, looking frightened.

'Right then, you stay here now, there's a good boy. Jack'll be OK. You stay here and I'll phone Will to come over for the milking. I'm sure he'll manage.' Shanco nodded. 'You feed the calves as usual and I'll be back as soon as I can.'

There was no time to explain anything else, and one of the men helped her climb up into the back of the ambulance. Jack was on his back, a blanket tight around him, one of the men pushing a needle into a vein on his arm. She noticed the marks from haymaking still scratching his skin. As the ambulance drew away from the yard, Martha watched Shanco through the back window, getting smaller: a tiny figure nursing Bob for dear life.

There was no siren; no point out here in the country with next to no traffic. She sat on the plastic seat, eyes fixed on Jack. A man in green uniform and white rubber gloves was sitting at her side, pulling some sort of mask over his face. Jack had worn a mask for harvest too, except there was a tube attached to this one.

'Don't worry, love, your old man'll be fine.' Martha decided not to answer him. 'Looks like he's had some sort of stroke. His breathing's stabilised now though, and he looks a strong 'un.' She observed the driver pulling faces at the other man in the mirror. 'Giving him a little oxygen now. It'll make it easier for him to breathe.' She nodded. 'So that was your little brother then! We were on the look-out for a kid, you see.'

Martha studied her hands. She noticed she was still wearing wellingtons and that they were caked in mud.

It took nearly an hour to reach the hospital: the men took Jack right in. She had to sit in a waiting room. It looked shiny, easy-wipe-down clean. A foreign-looking cleaner was buffing the corridor with a huge machine. There were other people waiting too: a woman holding onto her husband with a tight tight grip; an old man with a stick, and a mother in a baggy jumper with metal in her nose, her two small children sleeping stretched out on the benches. There were flowers on a table in the middle of the room, and a pile of pamphlets about all sorts of illnesses Martha had never heard of. She had only ever been twice to the hospital before now: both times with Mami.

It had changed a lot. Every now and then the others looked at her out of the corner of their eyes. Taking in every detail: the wellingtons, the dirty apron, her red cheeks. Time crept by; she couldn't stop herself looking at the door. Nobody. Martha went to look for a phone, dialled slowly, surprised at how much it cost now. She phoned Will, waiting a while for him to answer. He'd been outside, probably, and anyway he was going deaf. In the end he answered and promised to go over to Graig-ddu to do the milking. Martha explained about the red tape on the tails of the cows that had stopped giving milk, and that he'd need to watch out for that half-wild heifer. She even swallowed her pride and phoned Judy. Jack had given her Judy's number once, just in case, and she'd kept it in her purse. She didn't answer, though; just some English woman willing to take a message. Martha tried to explain but she ran out of money, even though a pound had gone in. She went to sit back down. A blonde head came around the corner.

'Martha?' She looked at her. A familiar figure offering a cup of tea. 'Remember me?'

'Gwen.'

'Yes; a bit older these days. Heard you were in here.'

'Oh,' she came to sit by Martha, gave her the cup, 'thanks.'

'Haven't seen you in years. Saw Jack's name on the list, see. Thought maybe you'd be here too.'

'Will he be OK?'

It was easier to ask her such a question as this, somehow: the question of a child. 'Well it's going to take a little while and a lot of work, but...' Gwen rubbed Martha's arm and for the first time in her life she felt comfort from another's touch. 'Don't worry, I've told the nurses on the ward to treat him like a prince, and to make sure he behaves!' Gwen's smile was infectious. 'And how's Shanco?'

'Fine; the same.'

'Used to have a lot of fun with him.'

'And how's your husband?'

'Fine. Still scratching a living in that garage. Our lad's got the farming bug, he's helping out at Faerdre Ucha at the moment. Getting married before long, don't know where the time goes.' A beep sounded somewhere from within Gwen's uniform. 'Oops, right then, better get going. Don't worry now; someone'll come and talk to you before long, then you can go and see him.'

Martha nodded and Gwen took her leave. Martha felt sorry she hadn't thanked her, as she watched the white back disappear through the doors.

'Mrs Williams?'

An efficient-looking nurse.

'Miss Williams.'

'Oh, sorry. Please come with me.' Martha followed the nurse along the corridor, feeling guilty as she trod on the newly-shiny floor. 'Right then, have a seat.' Martha sat down, her nails digging into the leather of her purse. 'Right then, your... um...'

'Brother.'

'Right, your brother. He seems as if he's had a stroke.'

Martha interrupted, 'So he'll not be able to work on the farm for a while?'

Strange question, thought the nurse, with the brother so ill. 'No, but we'll have to do further tests on him.'

'Right.' Martha knew that not being able to work the farm would be far more of a shock to Jack's system than any stroke.

'I can take you to see him now... and then I expect you might like to get home. He'll just be resting for a while now. Somebody's coming to get you, I take it?'

'Yes... of course,' Martha answered, with no clue as to who that might be.

She followed the nurse down the rabbit hole of a corridor. In a room at the far end was Jack. His clothes were in a plastic bag by the side of the bed; his muddy shoes in a separate bag. There were tubes in his veins and there was something on his chest which seemed to be counting his heartbeat, just like Martha had done in the field. His face was grey, his papery skin fit to ignite from the heat of his body. He had no sense of her being there, and Martha thought how small her big brother looked on the white bed. She went up close to him and the nurse drew up a little chair for her to sit by his side.

At Graig-ddu, Shanco had finished feeding the calves, and Will had done his best to milk the cows. He'd had to take his time because he hadn't used an old-fashioned milking parlour like this one since he was a lad working on some other farm. He was nervous about washing out the system afterwards, but he managed his level best. Jack had everything working well enough, but there hadn't been a penny more than absolutely necessary spent on the parlour in years. It was all old stuff, only just about good enough to get by with. Will could never understand why he didn't try and make life a little easier for himself, but Jack was old-fashioned like that. The rest of the world may have moved on years ago, but if that's the way things had been done at Graig-ddu, that's the way they'd always be run. He let the cattle out of the milking yard and moved the electric fence. Will left around eight, after looking at the livestock. He thought he should probably go and talk to Shanco, but he'd never been able to talk to him, not since he'd been little: it felt as though he were talking to himself.

Shanco tried to wait quietly for Martha in the house but he couldn't keep still. He was expecting Will to come and talk to him but he heard him leave, and by the time he'd run out onto the yard, the dust behind the Land Rover was rising halfway up the lane. Shanco wanted to see someone, talk to them.

144

He walked slowly back to Cae Marged and looked at the shape Jack's body had left in the barley. The ambulance tyre marks were still clear near the gate; so were the paths Shanco had beaten to fetch Martha and when he'd gone to the top of the lane. You could see the day's story mapped out in the barley where he stood. He looked up at the scarecrow and it looked back down at him with its crooked smile on its lolling head. Hatred burned suddenly in Shanco's chest, the hottest he'd ever experienced. He struck the scarecrow with all his force. He hit it as though it were a real man. He hit its belly until the straw burst out and its head hung low. He kicked the wooden cross until his feet hurt; he scratched it until his nails bled. His sobs were echoed by the crows' cries. He held his own head in his hands, as though he were pleading for mercy. Slowly, on his knees at the scarecrow's feet, he began to calm down.

It was getting cold. Shanco got up, dried his tears on his sleeve and looked around. It was still quite light. He made his way back to the yard, going past where Martha and he had been searching that morning for the calf. He stood watching over the gate. There, in the middle of the long grass, was the cow. It was standing quite still with a newborn calf shining like silver, suckling steadily on its mother's teats.

THIRTY-ONE

The barley got choked by weeds and slowly started to rot. There'd been no time to harvest it. Shanco watched it all spoiling and dying back. No one had asked him, but he took down the shattered scarecrow and carried it back awkwardly in a wheelbarrow to the storehouse. The scarecrow fell out each time the wheel got caught in potholes on the way. Martha was spending most of her time going to and from the hospital on the bus. She'd walk to the village or sometimes Emyr Shop would be so kind as to offer her a lift. They hadn't seen hide nor hair of Judy nor the 4x4 since Jack's stroke. Emyr put up a notice in the shop window and Martha found a part-time milker who had taken over all the farm side of things.

Jack was getting better slowly but he was rather vague, and his body refused to follow his own instructions. Sometimes he'd lose his temper and start shouting through the night, no matter he was keeping half the ward awake. At other times he'd ask the same question over and again, and forget people's names or talk about people long dead as if it were yesterday. Now and then, though, his mind was clear as a bell; you had to take each day as it came. Martha found the travelling hard; it was tiring, waiting for buses. The housework got neglected, and Shanco had started to withdraw into his shell; hardly talking to anybody.

Since Jack had neither pyjamas nor slippers, Martha had been in town shopping for them, and decided to come home and visit him that night instead. It was still quite early so she'd have the chance to do some cleaning, boil an egg for Shanco and try and bring him out of himself: she'd even bought mints for him. He was like a snail: touch the soft flesh and he'd coil back inside himself for days. Martha's back was aching as she rounded the corner into the yard. She froze in shock when she saw the 4x4 outside the back door. Shanco appeared with Bob at his heels.

'J... Judy's here.'

Martha walked straight past him and into the house. She nearly bumped into her at the back door. Judy was loaded up with bags.

'Oh, it's you,' Judy said.

The anger was stopping her breathe. 'Yes, it's me.'

'Just came to collect me stuff.'

'What stuff?'

'Just bits an' pieces. Thought you'd be at t'hospital.' Judy missed a beat. 'How's Jack?' She raised her eyebrows.

'What do you care? You haven't even been to see him!'

'Oh, c'mon, Martha.' Judy smiled.

'What?'

'Not exactly the Florence Nightingale type, am ah?'

Martha could have given her a slap then and there.

'What have you got in those bags?'

'Just some of me clothes an' stuff.

'And how are you going to get them home?'

'Well, I was thinking o' takin' the 4x4, seeing as it's mine an' all.'

'What?!'

Martha's ears were burning; a flush was spreading down her neck.

'I reckoned sommat like this'd 'appen.' Judy put the bags

down and took out some papers. She threw them down on the table in front of her. 'Go on then, Maaatha, if you don't believe me.'

Martha picked up the papers in trembling hands. The letter confirmed that Jack had put the car in Judy's name: and most of their savings from the business account. Her mind was running in all directions.

'But how could he – ?' Martha began.

'Well, put it this way,' Judy replied, studying her long nails, 'it's amazing the results you get from a bit o' feminine persuasion and a lot o' Bells. And when you think abou' what's due to me in terms o' *services rendered*, I reckon' we're abou' quits, don' you?'

Judy snatched the letter from her and picked up the bags.

'Wait a minute!' She grabbed Judy's arm, realising this must be the first time she'd touched her. Judy turned to face her with a warning look. Martha remembered Jack coming home late one night, the stink of whisky on his breath.

'I wouldn't do tha' if I were you,' Judy said, shaking her arm free, 'you don' wan' me to call t'cops, do you? I'll 'ave yeh up for assault.'

'But he's ill, and I need to go to the hospital all the time. What if he gets critical again?'

'Not ma problem, duck.'

Judy was turning to go.

'Wait,' Martha said, 'the ring. At least give me back the ring.'

Judy swung around slowly, enjoying every minute. 'What ring?'

'Mami's ring.'

'Oh, this old thing, like?' She held up one finger in the air, scrambled it off and waved the ring in Martha's face.

148

''Course you can 'ave it back.' Martha felt absurdly happy, as though the ring made up for all her other losses. ''Course you can, luv. Gimme fifty quid and it's yours.'

This time it felt like heartbreak. She had no choice. She groped for her purse helplessly. The money was no more than the rustle of paper as it changed hands: Martha couldn't see it for tears. Judy threw down the ring. Shanco was sitting by the fire, his eyes hidden in his hands.

'Well, I'd love to stay an' chat but got places to go, people to see,' Judy said as she tapped out of the kitchen for the last time.

Martha fingered the ring, seeing the colours and shadows in the gold. The metal had got thin as gilt from Mami's wearing it so long, even when she was doing the hard work on the farm. At least it hadn't broken.

As Judy drove past she didn't see beyond the barley field to where the old tent was; the bones of it, anyway. It had borne the brunt of wind and rain. The poles stuck out at all angles, like some old carcass worried by wild animals.

THIRTY-TWO

Jack came home just as autumn's flames licked the hedgerows orange and red. It was still warm; the leaves curled up dry in the air. Jack was lifted upstairs by the ambulance men. He was in Mami and Dat's bed to save him from Shanco's pestering. Shanco had gone very quiet when he'd caught a glimpse of Jack in the back of the van: this was the first time in a month he'd seen him. Will had promised to lend Martha his old Land Rover temporarily, but when he came to give her the keys, he told her he'd bought a new 4x4 anyway and didn't want to be seen driving that old scrapheap around the place. Martha just smiled as she pocketed the keys. Will seemed to have suddenly become a generous man: maybe it was something to do with him hearing Martha would be selling all the animals.

A stone or so lighter, and whiter for being away from the sun all that while, Jack really did seem like a different man. When Jack had looked towards him, Shanco had seen how half Jack's face had fallen away like a sack of wool, taking with it the right eye and cheek. His right arm was limp in his lap, like a sickle left to rust in the rain. He'd been taken upstairs in a special chair, swaddled in straps and blankets like a baby. Shanco had not spoken to him; Jack seemed hardly to know him. He certainly hadn't noticed the roses Shanco had picked that morning and set on Mami's dressing table. All that kerfuffle focussed on Jack and not even a glance cast his way: Shanco went into a sulk, going off to comfort Roy, who seemed to miss the old Jack as much as Shanco did.

Martha let Jack settle for a while before taking up his dinner. She warmed the soup in a cast iron saucepan. She opened the windows: Mami always did that when someone was ill. Martha had been thinking hard about the future: she had no choice but to sell all the animals and just keep tack sheep which would only stay on the farm for the summer. Judy had stolen the farm savings, but they had enough left to keep the three of them going, if they looked after the pennies. Shanco would have to pull his weight a bit more, that's all; she could keep an eye on the money herself. She stirred the soup to stop it burning; she buttered the cut side of a loaf from the dresser. The food went onto a tray and she carried it all upstairs, trying to ignore her niggling back which seemed to hurt more each day. She had to set it down a moment to pull open the door, bend down again and take the tray in. Jack was asleep so she put it down on a chair by the bed.

'Jack,' she whispered, touching his arm.

'Gwen?' His eyes opened, trying to focus on the face hovering inches above his. She waited. 'Gwen?'

'No, Jack. Martha.'

'Martha?'

'Come on, wake up and you can have a bit of dinner.'

'Dinner, yes.' Martha hooked under his shoulders and helped him sit up. 'Got to gather in the hay next, haven't we?'

She set the tray on his lap, put the spoon in his good hand. The nurse had told her she should make him do as much as he could on his own. But he couldn't manage some things yet, like getting washed, going to the toilet. She watched him try and aim the spoon at his mouth. He let go and it fell smartly to the tray, smearing soup over it.

'Fuckin' thing!'

Martha smiled as she wiped it up. Jack smiled back, his eyes coming into focus.

'W... w....' He was getting to sound like Shanco. 'Wh... where's Judy, Martha?'

She had managed to avoid the subject so far. Sometimes though she felt like just telling him straight how he'd been had: to scream it at him. I was right from the start, she was reminded every time she had to struggle with that old Land Rover and missed nipping around in the little car. I knew right from the start, she wanted to scratch the words right down his poor, floppy face. All that work over all those years.... She noticed Jack was waiting for her to answer.

'Judy had to go back to Leeds,' she stepped around the words, 'the eldest wanted to be nearer his father.' It was sunny outside. 'She came quite a few times to the hospital but you were asleep.' Her nails were pressing half moon shapes into her palm. She lifted her hand to show him the ring. 'Fair play, though, look; she brought this back.'

There was a new stillness in Jack's eyes, deep waters that Martha felt she could read as never before. She could see him trying to make sense of her words, like Shanco would, laying them out one by one like clothes put out to dry on the line.

'Thanks,' was all he said, looking at her sadly. She read his meaning in his eyes. He took the spoon again. She sat for hours to keep him company, loneliness stealing over her more than ever before.

That night Martha went to check Jack was sleeping before she put on her overcoat and stepped out. The nights were closing in on Graig-ddu like a cloak. It was clear; the cold had coaxed the leaves down, leaving the trees to lament their loss. There was a fine crop of nuts – Mami said that meant plenty of baby boys would be born – and blackberries bruising into purple fists.

Martha spent the afternoon arranging to sell the livestock: it would all go to mart within a week or so. She had thought about holding a sale on the farm, but she couldn't face all those people poking their noses into her business. She had to tell the milk company and the quota people; settle the bills – there was so much to do! The pressure had driven her out of the house.

She walked to the lane and followed her nose. Wandering through the garden, she looked at the roses that were beginning to wither away. The petals were strewn across the grass like confetti. Martha waited a moment, wondering. The washing up bowl was still on the wall; the familiar bushes retreating into shadows of themselves to withstand the winter. She thought of that fire she'd lit at the bottom of the garden, of Gwynfor's footprints, of the snowdrops and the bluebells. The crow came back to her too, and all those sleepless nights waiting for it to start up its knocking.

Her heart sank again and she flushed as she thought of something else. She'd had to tell the authorities about her brother; had to refer to him as an 'invalid', explain he couldn't work the farm any more. The word went up her spine step by cold step. In some people's eyes, it seemed that Jack had stopped existing, no more than Shanco had ever existed. Both were in-valid. She drew her coat closer around her. The business was in her name now too, since she was the only one who could make decisions any more. Somehow everything had landed in her lap just to slither away again. She breathed in the cold air as though it might bring her comfort.

She walked away from the garden and the yard, and up the lane, finding herself in Cae Marged. The barley lay flat on the ground, riddled with weeds, wet with mould: dank and smelly. She could smell the stink as she trod into the rot. Around the field she went, and over to the top hedge. The big oak had started to lose its leaves; white arms raised, it was pleading to the dark sky. She sat against the trunk and looked around. It would be Christmas again before you could turn round: she'd bring a wreath to the hedge right here as ever, and one to the graveyard. She thought about last year, how she'd cried like a baby. She turned towards the church: it looked back at her, its face serene. The tombstones shone like gemstones, but no tears came tonight: she was far too weary.

She sat quietly, looking out into the middle of the field where Jack had collapsed. She heard a rustle and saw Shanco out of the corner of her eye, tiptoeing through the long grass along the hedge. Martha saw that he'd been crying. He pulled from his pocket three kittens and placed them at her feet. Bob had been at it again. She looked at them in silence: one grey like mackerel with stripes around its little tail; the second sloe black; and the third, black with little white paws as though it had just stepped across snow. They hadn't even opened their eyes, not even caught a glimpse of this strange world before it was snatched away. Shanco was staring at them, sniffling. Just for a moment, Martha couldn't believe a mother in such circumstances would stubbornly stay on a farm that killed her offspring. Every litter met the same fate but still the cat stayed at Graig-ddu rather than finding some safe haven somewhere for her kittens. A bit like Judy, the cat could have adapted; would have survived anywhere with a scrap of food and a cuddle. She fell into contemplation of the kittens in the rotting field, and was almost surprised to hear herself start to speak.

'I had a baby once, Shanco.' He was startled. 'Well, for a little while anyway, I had one. Right here.' An owl hooted far away, and he turned away to where it came from, dark eyes darkening. 'It was Will's.' The words were far off somehow, 'and I had him here, just when we were about to sow the barley.'

Martha wasn't even listening to her own words. 'I was fifteen; I didn't even know I had him.' Shanco was looking at the kittens and saying nothing. 'He didn't live. But I didn't do anything to him. I held him close, close.' Shanco thought of a cradling that tight, and smiled. 'And then he was gone.' Shanco nodded. 'I didn't know what to do. Couldn't tell Mami, could I? I buried him here, in this hedge right here, and I went home to get washed. He was little, tiny: came too early, maybe. Will doesn't even know to this day, mind; no one knows.' The wind blew a lock of hair into Shanco's eyes. 'Should have had a baby with Gwynfor, see. But I could never leave Graig-ddu and leave him alone here now, could I? Don't think the little mite even cried.' Shanco pushed his hair away again. 'It wasn't the right time. I didn't want to do anything with Will: I had no choice.'

The words had dried hard inside Martha over the years; now she felt as though she were spitting out cherry-stones.

'I had no choice....'

She didn't need to say any more. She looked at the kittens with their eyes shut, and she picked one up on the palm of her hand.

155

Shanco listened out for the owl, watching her cuddling the kitten to her. His mind went back through the years to that day he saw Martha burying something under the oak. Once she'd run home, he and Jack went to see what it was. When they both saw what she'd buried, they buried it again and ran like wind through barley back to the storehouse to hide.

Martha and Shanco sat there for a moment, looking at the kitten. The owl hooted again. He turned back from listening to the low notes, and his broad smile lit up Martha.

THIRTY-THREE

Since she'd started looking after Jack full time, Martha was enjoying going to town even more than she had before. It was a relief to leave the farm behind, and now that he was starting to get better, she could take her time when she was there. The rain had draped in wet sheets around Graig-ddu, but despite this, things were better here than they had been for months. Jack watched the raindrops splashing in circles on his window, hoping he'd be up and about for Christmas. They'd agreed to move things around in Mami and Dat's room to make it more convenient for him. Martha was spending time up there with him, helping him exercise his arm and reading with him to strengthen his voice. Whether or not the extra attention made any difference, at least she felt she was doing something.

Martha paid over the odds to get the men from the mart to fetch the animals. She kept her distance until all the sheds were empty. She glossed over the details with Jack, so as not to upset him, casting a rosy light instead on the numbers queuing up to keep their tack sheep at the farm, and how she'd need his help to keep them in order. This morning, he had managed to feed himself: Martha felt at last she was getting some return from all that effort.

She brought down his breakfast tray and stood at the table, weeping. They were tears of thanks, and as she dried them slowly, she felt her burden begin to lift.

She got changed and put on her blue suit, smart for town.

She'd even got used to that great lump of a Land Rover, and she was looking forward to visiting Eurwen's café. Today she took her time, calling at the butcher's where she bought a steak for tea and a pound of mince. The butcher asked after her brother, suggesting a little red meat would do him the world of good. She picked up Shanco's tablets – and Jack's now, too – marvelling at the mountain of medicines she was hefting into the house these days. After the Co-op she parked the Land Rover carefully, locked the boot and went into the café. Martha was glad to see there was no one at her favourite table, and she sat down. She saw that the same old bored waitresses were waiting to serve. She took out her purse and went to order milky coffee and a cake. She chose a fresh cream cake with strawberries. She went to sit down and waited. She was disappointed how quiet it was in there today. Not that she'd ever talk to anybody, it was just that she liked to listen. She heard one of the girls behind the counter complaining that her husband spent all his time playing darts down the pub when he should have been home having his tea. Another agreed, saying she'd half a mind to refuse to make his tonight, since he was late so often most of his food ended up cold and in the bin.

The bell chimed as two women came in and sat around the corner from Martha. They settled down, all carrier bags and chit-chat.

'You know, I heard she took the lot. What an old fool. Serve him right.'

She felt her ears burning, but she'd no proof they were talking about Jack.

'Made herself scarce, she has; off to try it on the next soft old sod. But then I always said there was something odd about that family, didn't I? Keeping to themselves like that, who d'they think they are?'

The pair watched the waitress' movements as she brought Martha her coffee, their eyes eventually landing on Martha herself. Their faces fell; they rallied; they smiled and nodded. Hadn't named names, had they now? Martha was blowing on her hot coffee, determined to show a cool face to those two gossips, when the bell chimed again.

'Martha.'

She looked up, noticing the gossips' eyes on stalks.

'Gwynfor, how are you?'

'Fine!'

Martha put the cup back down on its saucer before her nerves set it chinking.

'Can I sit here?'

'Of course.'

He'd ordered his tea and was back before Martha had got over her surprise. One of the gossips was enjoying the scene behind her through the mirror of her compact. Gwynfor noticed too, raised his eyes at Martha. She smiled back weakly.

'Marth-'

'Gwyn-'

'Sorry.'

'You go first.'

'Martha, I'm sorry about your brother; I hope he's better.'

'He is getting better, thanks.'

'I'd call round, but you know how it is.'

'I know exactly how it is.'

Martha looked him in the eye. She'd never done that before, and Gwynfor shrivelled slightly under her gaze.

'Martha.'

The waitress brought his tea.

He was fishing for his words, which seemed to have dived beyond his grasp. 'This is where we first met, isn't it?' She nodded. 'I'm sorry, Martha. It wasn't supposed to turn out like this. I would have come and seen you but, well, by then it was too late.'

'And how are they; your wife and the little one?'

Her question shot straight down the aisle so that Gwynfor fell like a skittle.

'Oh, OK, thanks.'

'There's no need to feel guilty, you know. It was all my fault, the way I wouldn't leave the farm, and now it's too late.' He nodded. 'Things could have been different, but now I've got two brothers to look after, and you've got two of your own to think about now as well.'

He hadn't touched his tea. 'I never thought I'd be a father at my age.'

'That's the way things go sometimes.'

'One minute I was just visiting; the next I was married.'

'Fate, maybe.'

'Maybe.'

'Still, though; you're a rich man: got your own farm, plenty in the bank.'

Martha couldn't resist a hint that maybe he'd fallen into the same trap as Jack.

Gwynfor fiddled with his nails. 'She's a little girl; pretty, dark. I adore her.'

'And your wife? Get on OK, do you?'

'She's not the same...'

'Sh... that's enough, now, Gwynfor. I shouldn't have asked.'

'Not like...'

'Shh.'

A pause.

'And how's the piano?'

'Fine, thanks.'

'You play?'

'Yes, every night,' the lie slipped from her tongue. She didn't know where it came from: the same place as pride, perhaps. Or maybe she lied because she just wanted Gwynfor to have a picture of Martha at the piano, playing beautifully, when he was in the midst of his new, noisy family life.

'Right, best be off. She doesn't like me being late.'

'Of course she doesn't.'

'Thanks, Martha.'

He smiled at her and turned to go, the bell chiming his farewell. The gossips followed him out shortly afterwards, eager to spread the word.

Martha stayed a while in the café. Her coffee was quite cool enough to drink. A conversation like that would be enough to turn her stomach usually, but this had been different. She felt as though she'd shrugged off some weight, and she was glad she'd yielded nothing. On the surface she'd felt very little as she watched Gwynfor's back disappear behind the door's 'Open' sign. But there was some emotion lurking deeper, something she identified as pity. The sort of pity you feel for people you don't love. She nibbled at the cake, enjoying every crumb. She sighed with pleasure and went to pay. There was no point hanging around today: she had things to do. They'd have to make the bathroom and the stairs safer for Jack. She fancied a new blouse too: a lot of her old clothes were getting shabby, and that wouldn't do at all. Martha went out into the street and set about her business with a new resolve.

That morning, Shanco had watched Martha crying quietly in the kitchen after she'd brought down Jack's tray. He had looked at her through the window and watched her drying her tears. He'd pressed his nose against the glass, had hidden in a cloud of his own steamy breath. Then he'd hidden himself away behind the cowshed wall, and he'd watched her getting into that Land Rover awkwardly, drive away slowly up the lane. Shanco sat there shivering, his eyes staring into the far distance. The picture he was looking at was Martha's tearful face, and he could not get it out of his mind as he walked back to the house. He opened the back door slowly and he went in. He poured a glassful of milk and went up the stairs towards Jack's room; the glass in one hand, and in the other, the little white bottle with the yellow cap.

THIRTY-FOUR

By the time Martha got home, the night was closing in. She still couldn't get used to how empty the yard sounded now, without the pumping of the milking machine. The place was utterly quiet, utterly still without the calves' lowing in the stalls nor the milking cows grazing noisily nearby. She opened the boot of the Land Rover and unloaded her shopping bags. Among the usual items were clothes, and meat from the butcher's for tea. She slammed the door shut with her elbow. She heard Bob barking. She went into the kitchen. The fridge was open, the milk bottle left out. Shanco still hadn't got used to having his milk out of a bottle rather than straight from the tank in a jug. She'd have to tell him off for this. A tight collar of cream, formed in the heat of the room, was choking the bottle neck. She put down her shopping carefully by the sink and began to put things away. She'd have to think about getting tea ready soon. She hoped Jack fancied steak. She went out onto the doorstep to call Shanco to help her peel the potatoes.

'Shanco!' No answer. 'Shanco!!' Still no answer. 'Shanco, where are you then?'

There was only the sound of Bob barking, and Roy scratching at the door of his kennel. Martha returned to the kitchen and shifted the kettle to the hottest part of the hotplate. She opened the bag from the clothes shop and looked into it happily. She decided to go up and see if Jack was awake. She filled a glass with water for Jack. She carried it carefully in one hand, using the banister to keep her balance. She pulled herself up, reminding herself of all the people that had asked after him. She opened the door and stepped into the room.

She let go of the glass, which broke into a thousand stars across the floor.

'Jack!' He had kicked off the blankets. His face had frozen into a horrific expression; black liquid snaked from his mouth and onto the bedclothes. 'Jack!'

Martha touched him: his body was cold, heavy and was not its normal colour. She lifted her hand away as if she'd been burnt. His eyes were staring back at her from a blue-tinged face. There was no life in his eyes, no depth. Jack had gone. Martha put her head in her hands. 'But... oh!'

Her heart was beating so fast she had to steady herself against the bedside chair. She looked down. There was another glass that had broken, and some milky liquid seeping across the floor, grainy with white powder. She had set out Jack's dinner by the bed. How did he get the milk? The answer came creeping up her spine.

'Shanco!'

She was looking around wildly, trying to fix her loss anywhere in the room except on Jack. She turned and ran downstairs. Her whole body was shivering and tears streamed from her eyes.

'Shanco!' No answer. She heard Bob barking again. 'Bob!' She turned full circle in the yard, confusion hemming in her thoughts. It was dark, and so still. In whatever direction Martha chose to step, she felt the ground beneath her sag. 'Bob!' As she tried to orientate herself towards the barking dog, shapes around the yard blurred as if she was moving at high speed. 'Bob!' The little dog barked again. She went over to the storehouse and up the slate steps, praying under her breath. 'Shanco!'

She felt that she was sleepwalking. The door opened. Martha fell to her knees. In the dark of the storehouse, Shanco's body was lying in the scarecrow's embrace. His eyes were as empty as his companion's. Black blood streamed across Shanco's chest, as it had from his brother's mouth. At his feet was Bob, healthy as ever, guarding the empty little bottle of poison.

The ambulance can't have had much problem finding the place this time. They gave Martha something to help her sleep, and they lay her down on the pink sofa in the parlour. The police arrived, swarming like flies around a corpse. The bodies were removed together, once the photos had been taken for the records. A social worker stayed on a few hours with Martha because the police were worried she'd no family to keep an eye on her. They tried to get her to stay somewhere else for a while, but she refused to leave Graig-ddu.

Later that next day Martha spoke to the police, and they phoned Gwynfor to confirm that she had been in the café; somehow they contacted those café gossips too and got the same story, so at least they did Martha a good turn in the end. Gwynfor, meanwhile, had to face a second set of questions from his wife, suspicious of him taking tea with another woman. Martha was questioned about where and how Shanco found the poison. But since the Strychnine had been so old, bought in the days when rules about such things were lax, and since it seemed that neither rhyme nor reason ruled Shanco's actions, the police decided he must have been set on killing Jack, by poison, or by any other means. There would have to be an inquest, naturally, but there was no doubt about what had happened.

Shanco must have seen Jack as being a bit like that cow with no teats: he needed a helping hand into a better place. He was strong; he could have easily overpowered him, got him to drink the poison. Maybe Jack just drank it all up, didn't notice anything wrong. The police said afterwards they could tell from the different times at which they died, that Shanco had stayed with Jack until he'd gone. Then he must have swallowed the rest in the bottle with a little more milk for himself; gone out to the storehouse, cradled that scarecrow. Martha had to block the details from her mind. The poison doesn't kill straight away, so they say: you can live up to an hour after you swallow it. It gives you convulsions that last so long it feels like that's all you've ever known. The death Jack had shared with Shanco was the slowest, the most painful, most horrific death you can imagine.

THIRTY-FIVE

Jack and Shanco were buried with the rest of the family in the church graveyard, by the top hedge looking over the farm. They were laid in the family grave, facing the opposite direction to all the others. It was a miserable morning: grey with rain threatening. There was no close family that might have come to the funeral. Martha had asked for a quick and simple service: it was all over in well under an hour. Emyr Shop was the only one there to hold her by the arm as they went along the winding walk arched with yews, shadowing the coffin. The men from the undertakers were the bearers. She looked beyond the church door and across the hedge, towards the fields of Graig-ddu and those of Will Tyddyn Gwyn. She could see a lonely figure there in the top field: Will training his sheepdog. Martha stopped and looked at him a moment. He looked so small to her from the churchyard: just some old, stooped stranger.

She was too far away to see the tears forming in Will's eyes as he sent the dog weaving back and fore like wind through barley. Emyr tugged her elbow to draw her attention back to where she stood. Martha didn't know, but Will had that morning, time and again, walked up to the top of her lane and back, in two minds as to whether or not to bring his condolences. As the vicar spoke the dismissal, Martha's mind was far away. Today up in Cae Marged field, the tack sheep were quietly grazing. But her mind's eye was fixed on the oak there, where another little body lay, on the boundary between theirs and Will's farm.

167

After the funeral, Martha climbed back alone over the hedge and home. She wouldn't accept a lift from Emyr, who watched her as she went, a small figure that had aged in a fortnight. He shook himself from reverie with the realisation he had to get back to the shop: people would be waiting to hear all about the latest news.

Martha pushed open the back door and bent to pick up the pile of cards. The paper in places was warped by the wet seeping under the door from days of rain. They were thrown, unopened, onto a pile with the rest on the dresser. She took off her black coat and undid Mami's brooch from her new blouse.

She made tea for herself, thinking how different Dat's funeral tea had been, the yard crammed with cars, the house thrumming with men in black like crows circling a shrine of stories. Mami had brought out the best china, and cakes had come from every corner of the county, as well as six cob-loaves sent courtesy of the baker. Mami's tea had been quieter; there were fewer friends and neighbours by then.

Martha sat at the kitchen table looking at the shroud of rain lowering outside. Her face was white like the moon against her mourning clothes. She heard Roy whining from his kennel. His howls had filled the yard for days, his claws scraping the door like that crow at their window. His food bowl lay untouched; not even a caress could comfort him. She had last night come close to striking him to get him to shut up, but she'd remembered Jack had said that was the worst thing you could do to a dog like Roy. Then again, Bob didn't seem to miss Shanco at all; he just carried on his sweet silly ways as if his master had never been. He was the only creature at Graig-ddu who seemed untouched by grief.

Martha couldn't eat, so she went out still wearing her

mourning clothes. The sound of her smart heels was sent echoing around the yard as she went towards the storehouse. She hadn't been here since she'd found Shanco. She walked slowly up the stairs, sorrow lending her a serene air she didn't feel inside. The stillness was a relief after the police and all the other strangers had crawled all over their little world. She sat on the top step, looking up at the church. Martha could see far tonight: rain must be on the way. The air was heavy, grey: sounds were carried far afield. She could see the church hedge like a dark line in the weak light.

Thoughts were flickering through her mind but it all seemed so far away. The cow with no teats; the bowl in the garden; the tent in the field; the crow; the cat; the rotting barley; the milk that hid the taste of poison; the little white bottle with its yellow cap. The pictures came into focus, and she started to understand Shanco. None of the symbols made sense, but they were filling her head with a glaring light. She rubbed her forehead.

That night she lay in bed. She couldn't sleep, even though grief had sucked the life from her. She sat up in bed, looking out of the window onto the yard. She had asked Emyr to board up the rooms belonging to Shanco and Mami and Dat, so that never in her life would she have to go back in there again. She watched the rain fall onto the yard. Wet rain falling like crystals from another world, shattering onto the slates. The yard was washed with grey; Cae Marged like slate in the distance. Martha imagined the oak in the dark with the wet stripping its branches of its last leaves.

It wasn't long before Christmas, when she would be having dinner on her own. She sat right up, leaned forward and reached out to open the window. The cold was like a slap;

169

the wind and the sound of crows came into the room. She kneeled up like a little girl at prayer. Mami's ring was safe on her wedding finger: she stretched it out to look at it. She was glad to hear the crows cawing. *That stuff will kill seven times over*. The words whipped in the wind around her, lifting the white of her nightdress into a ghostly silhouette. She started counting on her fingers. The crow; the fox; the magpie; the rabbit; Jack, and then Shanco. That made six. Martha let the damp wash her face quite clean; she felt the night come down upon her like a shroud. She counted again, and she smiled as she realised who would make seven.

ACKNOWLEDGEMENTS

Loving thanks are due above all to my mother, Caryl Davies, who edited two thirds of the book but died suddenly before we could complete our work together. Thanks for lending me those dictionaries in secret.

Thanks also to my father, Gareth Alban Davies, to Diarmuid Johnson and to Sioned Rowlands who all looked over the text; to Simon Thomas, who is very good on folklore; to Francesca Rhydderch for her encouragement, and to Caryl Lewis herself for her support.

Lastly, thanks to all at Parthian.

GD

PARTHIAN Fiction

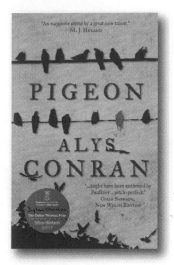

Pigeon

Alys Conran
ISBN 978-1-910901-23-6
£8.99 • Paperback

**Winner of Wales Book of the Year
Winner of Rhys Davies Award**

**'An exquisite novel by a great new
talent.' – M.J. Hyland**

Ironopolis

Glen James Brown
ISBN 978-1-912681-09-9
£9.99 • Paperback

**Shortlisted for the Orwell Prize
for Political Fiction**

'A triumph' – *The Guardian*

**'The most accomplished
working-class novel of the
last few years.'** – *Morning Star*

PARTHIAN   Fiction

The Levels

Helen Pendry

ISBN 978-1-912109-40-1

£8.99 • Paperback

'...an important new literary voice.'
– Wales Arts Review

Shattercone

Tristan Hughes

ISBN 978-1-912681-47-1

£8.99 • Paperback

On *Hummingbird*:
'Superbly accomplished... Hughes prose is
startling and luminous' – *Financial Times*

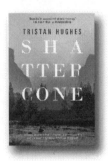

Hello Friend
We Missed You

Richard Owain Roberts

ISBN 978-1-912681-49-5

£9.99 • Paperback

'The Welsh David Foster Wallace'
– Srdjan Srdic

The Blue Tent

Richard Gwyn

ISBN 978-1-912681-28-0

£10 • Paperback

'One of the most satisfying, engrossing and
perfectly realised novels of the year.'
– *The Western Mail*